Rapid Transient

Steve Anderson

See Breeze Press

Cover Art by Kristi Jorgensen

ISBN-13: 978-0615642420
ISBN-10: 06156424X

seebreezepress@gmail.com

For Jane and Earl

Rapid Transient

1

I came to Great Valley not by choice, but on the chance there might be a job opportunity on the distant horizon. And I wound up in this boom-gone-bust town where things were starting to happen again. There was talk of gambling being a possibility to boost the local economy, and more than enough drilling for natural gas from wells nestled among the sagebrush and shale in the harsh and sparse landscape on the Western Slope of Colorado.

It was late May and the temperature was steadily rising. As I drove into town, a news blurb on the radio reported that it was supposed to be the hottest year on record. The reason, said the announcer, was due in part to global warming and a ten-year drought cycle.

But the air-conditioned lobby was cool and check-in at the Lucky U Motel was easy. Easy on the eyes, that is. She stood at about five-six, medium build with jet-black hair and a knockout smile. Her tight-fitting blue jeans outlined shapely thighs and the cowboy boots she had on gave her extra lift. She

1

wore a black blouse with cleavage holding firm in the low v-cut as she leaned over the counter top and wrote the room number on the registration card and slid it my way. "You need to fill this out."

After putting down the customary information I handed it back. "Got a weekly rate?"

She went down the card with her pen, checking each category. "So you're from Las Vegas? What a coincidence, the guy in the room across the hall from you is from Vegas, too. It's two-fifty a week."

"Such a deal. I'll take it," I said, not knowing at the time checkout would be a lot harder.

"Just let me know if you need anything . . . Uh, Wilfred Spiver," she said after reading the plastic I used to charge the first week's rent.

"It's Wily. Wilfred's an alias the credit card company somehow got a hold of."

"I'm Lucy." She reached out to shake my hand. "How long you planning on staying?"

"Haven't figured that one out yet." I answered truthfully, but she shot me a puzzling look. "I mean it depends on the job situation."

"Doesn't it, though? It's something everyone has in common when they come here expecting to make a decent living." She went back to perusing the registration card then paused long enough to give me a wary stare. "So what do you do?"

"Not making a decent living as a newspaper reporter. But there's a position at the *Great Valley Beacon* that might improve the situation," I said. "I hope to be staying longer than a week ."

"A town needs a decent reporter who's not afraid to write about the way things are around here."

"Yeah, don't all towns."

2

She slid the plastic through the card reader. "Tell me about it," she said and smiled while handing me the receipt. "Or stop by later whenever you get the urge, and I'll tell *you* about it."

I sauntered up the staircase, mulling over Lucy's remarks, then down the hall toward room 214. The lighting above produced a white, fluorescent haze, which made the red carpet look pale and gave the feeling of walking the length of a singlewide trailer. The dark wainscot paneling had begun to peel away from the wall like another layer of my life, exposing raw texturing in need of repair.

I had never been a roughneck or miner, but my acquired taste for an unassuming lifestyle came from working as a newspaper hack throughout the southwest, including Las Vegas. While pursuing a journalistic passion, I frequently looked for something that didn't require damage deposits, purchasing furniture, signing leases or any other long-term commitments. You get what you pay for, and by the looks of things the price could be very steep in places.

After settling in, I went down to the lobby. Lucy sat at her post behind the registration desk and gave me a quick history lesson in local politics regarding the *Beacon*. "There was this county commissioner who torched his own house. He was burning up his ex-wife's clothes and her other personal things in the fireplace when it got out of control. It should have been ruled an arson. Christ, everybody in town knew what happened." Lucy paused to light a cigarette. "But some reporter at the *Beacon* quotes the commissioner, like he's some kind of voice of authority, that it was caused by a faulty smoke stack.

The guy collects a shit pile of dough from the insurance company. What a crock! You know the *Beacon*'s motto? The Guiding Light of Truth."

I said, "Which commissioner was that?"

"Doesn't matter. They're all slimy weasels for the most part. He shot his wad and split town. Like everybody else when their luck runs out around here."

"Sounds like a familiar refrain; like there's no use dwelling on the past," I said and left it at that. But I could tell she didn't want a vague retort by the incredulous look she gave me.

"Uh, I'm talking about now, how the commissioners in this county operate. They're lining their pockets at the expense of the taxpayer. People're pissed off and it's not just about the greedy bastards making a killing, but because they're creating an environmental catastrophe in the process. Everything I read in the paper suggests a certain level of corruption that is just frickin' intolerable. Like this wacky scheme a Las Vegas developer came up with to sell Great Valley's water to some resort in Nevada when we're in a God-forsaken drought. Hell, we don't even have enough water to do laundry most of the time." She laughed at that. "Ha, ha, just kidding. Don't worry; you get clean sheets and towels — just not every day. You'll love it around here. Back to what I was saying, out here people kill people over water. Call it a sign of the times, but you gotta wonder if the last drop will be over water or blood. Read it somewhere like the *Beacon*."

The history of the atom bomb, gambling and water wars were three things I remembered most growing up in Vegas—in that order. "Shit is always hitting the fan where I was raised," I said. And it did in Great Valley, too shortly after my little celebration with Lucy.

I could tell that I was going to like Lucy, not only because of her shapely looks but because of her candor. I tend to judge women by whether they're real or phony. However, my lack of judgment in the past also steered me in a direction of reality that came close to dangerously lethal.

* * *

It started the next day when I found the offices of *The Great Valley Beacon* along Progress Avenue in the heart of downtown. The street was the main artery of the half-abandoned, former oil-shale town situated below the towering, bone-white Bookcliffs, ranging over a hundred miles.

I met Jeannette Lebreeze, managing editor of the *Great Valley Beacon,* and publisher, Rusty Gates, when I walked into the *Beacon* and applied for a job. They told me there was an immediate opening, and after providing an application and resume I was hired on the spot.

"Welcome aboard, Wily," said Rusty Gates. He was a big burly guy with a beard, wearing pressed blue jeans with a white shirt, and cowboy boots stuck in the air. He was reclining in a plush office chair behind a big desk, resting his legs on top. And I noticed the coat rack behind him had a cowboy hat and a black leather jacket hanging on it. "We've been a little short-handed these days, so you'll be a great addition, I'm sure. Your predecessor said he couldn't hack it anymore, but I thought he was a slacker and a wuss, tell you the truth. It can get kinda rough on reporters around here." He had a sort of Oakie accent with a bit of drawl but claimed he was from Nevada, like myself.

"Great to have you with us, Wily," said Jeannette and smiled, her deep blue eyes gazing at me. We were sitting in front of the desk, facing Rusty Gates.

Gates saying, "We gotta hell of a lot a work lined up. Hope you're ready to kick some butt."

"It's been one of my strong points, Rusty. Count me in. I've been living out here my whole life. I can handle it."

"Yeah, looks like you got some history, that's why I hired you." Rusty looked at me suspiciously and said, "It's a probationary thing you gotta get past, you know, standard pro-cedure around here. The bright side is you git a raise in thirty days."

He sifted through a pile of papers, looking for something in particular. When I looked at Jeannette she was rolling her eyes and shaking her head. "Rusty, if you're looking for the list of story ideas, it's on my desk. When we're done here I'll fill Wily in on the assignments," she said, then smiled at me. "Wily, if you'll follow me back to my desk we'll go over the details and get you started tomorrow, first thing."

We all stood up and shook hands. Rusty with his solid grip and broad shoulders had about three inches on me and was about thirty pounds heavier.

Jeannette LeBreeze was slender with long brown hair that fell into a wave below the shoulders. She wore a denim skirt and white blouse cinched at her narrow waist with a Concho belt, considered the

Santa Fe look in some circles, or country peasant in others. A charming style, to be sure.

She was quite spectacular from the rear as well. I watched her quick gait glide along on hardwood floors, tap dancing through the office building, which was sectioned off into various departments. Past the reception area there was advertising and production, then editorial. We went through the back door, out across the alley, where Jeannette showed me the workings of an outdated press being attacked by two guys named Butch and Marc. Their faces and arms smeared with black ink and sweat, they looked like coal miners in dirty tee shirts, sort of blending into the dark spaces of the old garage instead of a mine.

"Hey," said Butch with a wrench in his left hand while shaking my hand with the other.

"Hey," said Marc, emerging from between the rollers of the press.

"Hey, guys. Are we going to have it working before tonight's run?" asked Jeannette nonchalantly, then she stood off to one side of us, inspecting the decrepit machinery bathed in white fluorescent glow.

"Sure," they assured her. Then Butch added, "But it's kind of sketchy if we can't get them parts ordered before it breaks again."

Jeannette said, "Pretty soon you won't have to worry about any of those things. It'll all be on the net. And won't that make your day."

* * *

Feeling the need to celebrate, I bought a bottle of champagne at a small liquor store next to the motel and headed back to my room, thinking to myself it would be fun to share the moment with Lucy. But she was helping a guy at the counter when I came in. At first I thought she was ignoring me until she glanced at the bottle I was holding high in the air. A business type wearing a sport coat was bending over filling in the registration info when Lucy gave me the thumbs-up from behind the counter. The guy was either oblivious I was behind him, or didn't care.

"That'll be ninety-five a night," she told him flat out.

"Pretty steep for a business rate," he said. "You know it's worth half that."

All I could see was his back but you could tell the guy was a pompous twit just by the tone of his voice.

"Our rates vary depending on the season. Right now they're high."

"Why, because you're about the only game in town when everything else fills up? Anyway just give me the key and my credit card back." When he turned to see me glaring at him, he added with a sarcastic grin, "Yeah, it's what I've come to expect around here. Great hospitality and a courteous staff." He brushed me aside while heading toward the stairs.

I glanced at a disgruntled guy wearing his Oxford dress shirt with tie and sports jacket. He had short black hair and a thin dark mustache. From what I could tell he was out of style for a town that dressed mostly in jeans and tee shirts.

"Nice guy. It must be customer appreciation day, because you should've charged him double. But it's not my place to tell you how to run your business," I said after he was out of earshot.

8

"It's not my motel. I just work here. I do have some leeway since my stepfather owns it though. Anyway, the guy's a prick. He's one of those Vegas types who's been staying here off and on the last couple of weeks working on some hush-hush deal about a leisure community project and gambling hall. But nobody knows for sure since there hasn't been much in the paper about it," she said while filing paperwork into a drawer below the countertop. "Besides, the high-roller hasn't ever tipped any of the maids that I know of."

It was nearing twilight as shadows from beyond the plate-glass window darkened the lobby and lounge area, softening the atmosphere to where it almost looked plush in the shabby lobby stuffed with outdated furniture and worn carpet.

After pausing a moment to take in the ambiance, I said, "Since he's getting a pretty good price by sticking it to the help, he shouldn't complain."

"He's been a hell of a guest. I wish he would take his business elsewhere, but if I said anything it'd be considered discrimination and the old man would get sued by some shyster lawyer from Vegas. Speaking of which, that was him you just passed."

"How do you know?"

"Just look at those beady eyes when he stares at you. He seems to either want to intimidate or manipulate, you know? I haven't decided if he wants to screw me or sue me. Probably both at the same time, you think?" She laughed, and then added, "Besides he's part of the legal team representing the Vegas developer Victor Saville. Mr. Vito Manatelli was the one whose presence you graced."

"What room's he in?"

9

"Down the hall from you. But it's Saville you want to meet. The man with the plan who does all the talking. He's your neighbor directly across the way. The nicest suite in the house and he always reserves the room in advance. But they generally don't stay more than a couple of days at a time. Personally, I like Saville. We've sort of become friends. But I hate his politics and what he stands for."

I offered her some champagne but told her the glasses were back in my room. She went into the office behind the counter and produced two coffee mugs and said she'd have a small cup while waiting to see who else needed a room for the night.

We sat on the sofa in the small lounge area while I poured both of us some bubbly and she turned on the table lamp. Not nearly as romantic as I had envisioned but comfortable, reminiscent of a frat house living room.

Then she started humming away until breaking out in song. Something like an old Patsy Cline song ". . . crazy for loving you," she sang, and then followed with an upbeat Stevie Nicks from an early Fleetwood Mac tune.

"Amazing voice you have," I said, "it's kind of mesmerizing." I meant it too. It was melodious and soothing at the same time.

"Thanks. My mom used to be a singer with a country western band back in Oklahoma City where I originally came from. She sang and my dad worked in the oil patch until they got a divorce after moving to Great Valley. Dad was looking for that same stinking patch, only it was natural gas this time. Then she married Great Valley's grand entrepreneur, Eloy

10

Munn, for money. She sure as hell wasn't going to get any singing gigs in a town like this."

Lucy sipped on her mug and explained how things were starting to happen again in Great Valley. "Take Vic Saville for instance. He shows up with the latest dream of a large resort with a big lake surrounded by condos and a golf course. You know, all the amenities in your usual desert community, including hotel and casino. Thing they don't tell you is it'd really be a reservoir for water storage for an even bigger resort down river in Nevada. Course it all hinges on a special election for the gambling initiative. If the town approves it, there would not only be homes, but hotels and casinos on the open range. I've been in this town most of my life and it's always the same old shit, but with a different scheme," she said. "Before, it was uranium, then oil shale and natural gas. The list goes on. Everybody looking to cash in on real estate."

* * *

What little I knew about Great Valley I discovered online before driving the three hundred miles through southeast Utah to the little town surrounded by towering cliffs to the north and a ragged mountain range to the south. Below Great Valley, and atop the ten thousand foot Bookcliff precipices, sat the Naval Oil Shale Reserves. What the Navy didn't own, Omni Oil Corporation purchased, or permanently leased from the federal government in a hopeless attempt to extract oil from the massive rock pile. The failed effort had created yet another localized depression the Western Slope

11

town had grown accustomed to throughout the decades.

Despite the glut of housing and commercial spaces, Great Valley didn't dry up and blow away, but was starting a revival of sorts with a natural gas boom. But, the economy had shifted and people were thinking again of bailing out.

However, it had survived past boom and bust cycles. Earlier on, another Great Valley employer, Union Carbide, shut down after it quit processing vanadium and uranium for atomic bombs. The only thing blowing in the wind then was the plant's toxic yellowcake dust from the mill tailings, which also created jobs once the hazard was declared an EPA Superfund Project. The waste, including parts of the production plant, was moved twenty miles north of town to a burial site lined with bentonite.

* * *

The day after being hired, I covered the commissioners' meeting, where Victor Saville and environmentalist Derrick Banyan first clashed. Saville was promoting his lakefront resort: "It's a leisure community with an 800-acre reservoir," he told the commissioners. "It'll provide a steady stream of jobs, tourists and retirees, while offering multiple recreational opportunities, like an 18-hole golf course, fishing and water skiing."

"In your dreams," the environmentalist Derrick Banyan had shouted at the three commissioners and Saville, who stood before the commissioners at the podium. "Not in a million years has there ever been a large body of water in the Sorrow Creek Basin. It is

12

an extremely arid place prone to extended periods of drought. For the past ten years the highest water levels have only been two-thirds of normal at best. And you want to dam what little remains. That's crazy. You're insane if you think there's enough water for an 800-hundred acre reservoir. All I can tell you is, it ain't happening on my watch." Banyan stood among an audience of about twenty ranchers, businessmen and young people with long hair. In one final act, he held his hands in the air, palms up, gesturing like: 'what don't you get about this scenario?'

"Derrick Banyan, is it?" Victor Saville turned to face the crowd, took a deep breath, then added, "It actually works to everybody's benefit, Mr. Banyan. Storing water will help alleviate the current drought conditions in the region. And will be environmentally sound for a variety of species, including agricultural types."

The audience stirred some, murmuring among themselves. In a sense it sparked people to life, including the commissioners, who whispered to each other beyond the microphone's reach. All three were cattlemen of sorts. But mostly, I'd come to find out later on, they were full-time business leaders.

Saville turned to the audience, smiled, and said, "When presented with these basic facts, you'll be interested to know Omni Oil Corp., whose oil shale division owns all the water rights to the head waters of Sorrow Creek, has agreed to lease the water to Nevada Resorts International. After constructing the reservoir, the additional water storage would also help in the expansion of a small community down river next to Las Vegas. In the event that oil shale is

13

a viable resource in the future, then Omni would have the reservoir already in place for its operations, saving millions of dollars in the long run."

Great Valley commissioner Wayne Baxtrum sat on the bench between the two commissioners and basically agreed with Saville, saying, "So the benefits outweigh any sort of impact the development would have on an environment that is essentially considered a wasteland to begin with."

But Derrick Banyan wasn't buying it. Since he was a renowned environmentalist, he repeatedly attacked the proposal to the point of eventually being denied further comments by the commissioners. After saying for the record, "My primary concern is preserving Sorrow Creek's sensitive ecosystem from a water diversion project," he concluded with, "Any commissioner supporting this proposal will be recalled."

I had been taking copious notes throughout the meeting, ready to piece the story together on my laptop. However, when I returned to the room, concentration competed with exhaustion and noise from across the hallway. Almost winning the battle was a strong desire to have a scotch and flick on the tube. I was about to concede to the scotch but thought twice about the early morning deadline, which drew ever closer, as indicated not by any majestic rose-colored sunrise, but glowing red digital numbers on a clock radio signaling dawn's approach.

As I was wrapping up the story of an optimistic future for Great Valley, loud thuds shaking the thin walls drew my attention to the peephole, where I observed the once contained pandemonium spill into

14

the hallway. I was pissed off enough at losing my thought process to finally intervene. I opened the door.

"What the hell's going on?" I shouted as I caught sight of Victor Saville gripping Derrick Banyan's shirt collar. Banyan was pinned against the wall, until he pushed free and stood erect, tilting his head slightly so as to part his long gray-streaked hair to one side.

Saville shot me a sidelong, savage look between his strands of oily black hair. "What the fuck do you want?"

"Just about to ask you the same question. I thought I heard someone knocking." I stood in the doorway, wishing I had a big stick in my hand instead of a doorknob.

"Aren't you the reporter from the meeting tonight?" Saville demanded.

"Wily Spiver from *The Beacon*. I wanted to get you and Mr. Banyan to clarify a few things earlier, but it looked like you were too busy. Now that you're both here maybe we could set the record straight"

"I got nothing to say that concerns you or your newspaper, except this is off the record." Saville depressurized slightly by straightening his tie and shrugging in his dark pinstriped suit coat. With a contemptuous sneer, he added, "Mr. Banyan and I were engaged in a friendly disagreement that has just been settled. Right, Banyan?"

Banyan looked slightly rattled, but remained undaunted by Saville's threatening demeanor. With a wry smile, he said, "Spiver, let's not make this part of the commissioners' story, agreed?"

15

They turned to face one another while I receded slowly back into the room and shut the door tightly. I locked it by hooking a small chain into its flimsy slot. But the only thing stopping anybody from entering would be me. There were muffled tones from the aftermath of the brawl as their ambiguous voices mixed with the heavy, hollow stomping of footsteps that moved further down the hall and then faded into oblivion. I went back to the commissioners' story, but eventually slid the laptop to one side and slumped over in a heap, trying to recall happier thoughts.

I made deadline with the lead story. But any lucid details of the fight I briefly witnessed at the motel had long since evaporated with the heat of the next day. That is, until I went over to the cop shop to do my first daily ritual of scrolling through the police blotter. A short description of an argument at the Lucky U Motel caught my attention. An officer had issued a written warning for disturbing the peace to Victor Saville and Derrick Banyan.

I asked the dispatcher for the full report, which was usually kept from reporters in the event that something might be exposed to public scrutiny. Since the local cop shop was traditionally a tightlipped organization, they didn't believe in the public's right to know anything right away. "Under investigation" went a long way in concealing facts legally.

The dispatcher, a short redhead in her forties named Rita MacLean, sat silently behind the wall of bulletproof glass and in front of a 911 control panel with all the bells and whistles of a 747 bound for distant places. I figured, when she indicated any additional information would have to come from Chief Higgins, that part of her job was to say as little as possible to reporters. So I took a seat and waited.

Within five minutes Rita's voice crackled from the chrome vent-like microphone device attached to the thick window. "Chief Higgins said he'll get back to you later." The words echoed off the walls of the reception area, a small, nondescript room no one wanted to hang out in for very long. There were no magazines, like *Reader's Digest*, *Sports Afield* or *Popular Mechanics*, but instead a load of brochures on abuse prevention programs, as if clients of this institution were into getting educated after the fact, if for that matter, reading was even an option.

"When's that, did he say?" I asked, distracted by a black silhouette of a man towering over a screaming woman on the cover of a domestic violence flyer. Rita glared as if I were her main abuser in the sanctum of the cop world.

"He's on his way out and didn't say when exactly," she said. Then, as if by magic, Higgins appeared in the waiting area, shaking my hand and introducing himself. "Nice to meet you, uh . . ."

"Wily Spiver with the *Beacon*. Just hired, and this is my first assignment. I was hoping to get a chance to talk to you. If I could have just a moment of . . ."

"Wily, I'm on my way to a meeting. It'll have to wait." He said it with an air of authority that could knock the wind out of a person. A burly guy, about six-two with a cowboy hat. He stretched out his arm and firmly gripped my hand. "We'll have a little chat later on. Get to know one another."

"Great. I'll be at the office for the rest of the day." I left with little hope that I'd hear from Chief Higgins before we went to press. Although that proved to be the case, by the following day a much bigger story emerged about Derrick Banyan that paled in comparison to the hallway brawl.

That was when I began to pick up the thread leading to the web of things to come. It happens occasionally, where seemingly random stories begin to have significance; when fragments of a story start to emerge in such a way as to reveal the broader picture of things to come. And it happened when a Las Vegas developer and a radical environmentalist got together in a room full of politicians.

2

News of Derrick Banyan's accident wasn't brought to my attention from a simple police report, like most car crashes I had written about. It happened shortly after I left the office.

As I walked along Progress Avenue I heard a helicopter and its reverberations off the surrounding hillsides. The repetitive thud and distinctive rumble of a modern day meat wagon whirled above me and was about to drop from the night sky with all the force of a hovering gunship. Apparently the chopper ran frequent missions to Great Valley, picking up the severely wounded from Alden Memorial Hospital just up the street, and flying them seventy miles west to a trauma unit in Crescent City. The usual victims were survivors of car wrecks, heart attacks, gunshot wounds, or other causes associated with living in a mid-sized, western boom and bust town.

Since I was still wholly intact and not about to be whisked off to the heavens, I thought about celebrating life at the Portal Bar. After all, there was a sign; it hung above the barroom door with the motto: 'No Whimpering'.

I had just met Jim Tucker for the first time that day. The Tuck Man, who was the paper's photojournalist, took up residence on the stool to my right. He had been with the paper a little over a year, and told me to always talk to Red the bartender, since he knew about everything in town before it was printed.

"Hey, Tuck, did you pick up anything off the police scanner about an incoming chopper?" Tucker had a clean-cut, serious demeanor. He had reluctantly agreed to have one drink at the Portal Bar after work. Then he wanted to go home to his wife and kids.

Red cruised over when he heard 'chopper'. It appeared Red joined everybody's conversation, but kept a healthy distance, especially from unknown reporter types. "Unless he knows you, he won't talk to you," Tucker had said.

Red drew two more drafts from the tap and murmured, "Yeah, what's up with that?"

When Tucker settled down with beer in hand, he said, "There was a rollover near Banyan's ranch. Must have been pretty serious by the sound of it. But they never said who it was or the cause." Red suddenly became uninterested and walked toward the preferred clientele at the other end of the bar. "I didn't want to mention anything with Red listening. It would be old news before tomorrow's edition hit the streets."

I said to Tucker, "I thought you work things out with Red."

"Yeah, but mostly when it suits him. What do you say we take a ride out to the accident scene?" said Tucker. "We'll make it quick, maybe even faster than when Red finds out."

We swung by the office in my aging '96 Trans Am I called the Black Shadow to pick up Tuck's camera gear, then we rushed along five miles past the outskirts of town, but still within city limits.

"So Tuck, why the miles of empty space and we're still technically in town?" I said, then shifted into fourth to gain speed on the frontage road next to the interstate.

"Guess you haven't got around to reading Omni Oil's white paper on the area. Great reading."

"What white paper? I said, pondering the implication."

"It's Omni's master plan when oil shale is in full production." He was looking out into darkness, a few farm houses twinkling like sodium vapor stars on the horizon. "The town annexed all of this along the interstate believing there would eventually be about half a million living here by now, maybe more. The white paper said it all."

Then the night sky was filled with the flashing blue and red of two police cruisers that straddled the roadside. A fire truck was parked perpendicular to the road, blocking a small line of cars from proceeding further.

I rode the shoulder, passing several cars on the right, up to a firefighter and stopped. The guy in a red bucket helmet and yellow fluorescent one-piece suit was under orders to stop traffic. It didn't matter though, since we were already at ringside. Tucker emerged from the passenger side with camera in hand and started snapping away.

I searched the crowd for Chief Higgins. He seemed to have an elusive quality to his personality. Higgins had been invisible all day when I needed his comments earlier, but that night I easily spotted him. He was looking down at a crumpled pile of blue steel and chrome, reflecting artificial daylight from the halogen beams of an emergency vehicle.

Trying to catch his attention, I yelled, "Chief Higgins." He looked up, annoyed, but waved me over anyhow. "Any idea who it was? And what caused the accident?" I had whipped out my notepad to capture the customary quotes.

All I got was the lifeless phrase frequently relied on to describe a single-car crash. "Derrick Banyan. He might have lost control of the vehicle, but we'll be looking into the actual cause. I'll let you know what we find out," he said, then started off in the direction of a tow truck maneuvering into position.

The ride back to town was somber. Covering accidents was my least favorite part of a reporter's job. In the dark confines of the 'Shadow', Tucker asked me what the chief had said.

"Said he'd fill me in after the preliminary investigation."

"You'll have to bug him early. He hardly ever returns calls unless he wants the paper to cover some community program or a drug bust that makes his department look like they are saving the town from ruin." Tucker eased into the shadowed corner against the door and added, "Or if he thinks you know something he'd like in on."

Since we were on the subject of the chief, I asked Tucker if he had heard anything about a fight at the Lucky U Motel the night before involving Banyan.

"I thought that was your territory, Spiver, since you live there," said Tucker.

"True enough. I witnessed a portion of the brawl in the hallway, but fell asleep for the main attraction when the cops arrived. I'm still on hold for the blow-by-blow report from Higgins."

"Most likely Saville and Banyan couldn't agree on who was the bigger asshole," he said then quieted down, almost to the point of deep respite. Miles later, he reflected on Banyan. "Sometimes he doesn't know when to keep a lid on. It's not that I disagree with him or his politics, which I usually support wholeheartedly. Helluva generous guy too. He's given me a lot to write about. And I hate to say this, but he's such an extremist about everything, you know, pushing people's buttons with his personal agenda and all. Some of it's over the edge."

"I guess being green means sticking your point in someone's craw. Victor Saville must have had a big dose of it judging by the brawl in the hall."

"There's a benign maliciousness to Banyan," Tucker said. Then he let out a sigh, as if remembering some unpleasant exploits about the environmental crusader he'd covered.

I pulled up to the Portal where Tucker's car was parked out front. "How about a quick drink in mourning Derrick Banyan's condition?"

"And to all the great memories of Banyan's battles," Tucker said.

At the round table in the further recesses of the bar sat Victor Saville and two commissioners. We sat at the bar and watched them through the smoky mirror. "They're a rather jovial group, wouldn't you say, Spiver?"

"If I didn't know better, I'd think they're celebrating something." And as I said it, the three of them, as if on cue, raised their drinks in a toast. "Maybe Saville's wish came true now that Derrick Banyan is no longer on the scene."

"You couldn't possibly think Saville or the commissioners had anything to do with Banyan's accident?" He said it mockingly, but also with an element lingering in the air. "Good thing I'm not a betting man or I'd wager that Saville had something to do with it."

"I wouldn't bet against you even at a hundred-to-one. But for the moment it's still got to be written about objectively. At least the first time around."

Tucker eventually tuckered out and went home. I thought about heading back to the office to catch up on tomorrow's work overload, but after two more beers I found that the celebration of life also has its price. However, it still felt better than hearing some chopper hovering like a vulture overhead. I headed home to my wifeless motel room.

* * *

The *Beacon* was a daily paper, but I had already amassed several stories for the Thursday edition. Jeannette LeBreeze was not only in charge of managing the editorial and production staff, but kept the *Beacon*'s web page updated with news spots.

Jeannette didn't want the onerous task of reporting on Derrick Banyan's car accident, which had resulted in his being comatose. She stood at my decrepit wooden desk and told me so.

"I'm glad you're covering those gory details. My heart's just not in it," she said, gazing down at me when I swiveled the chair to face her. "I had a hunch something bad was going to happen to Banyan, but I didn't think it would be by accident."

"What do you mean?"

She said, "Banyan's crash took some in the community by surprise, but rumor has it he was probably run off the road by one of his many indigenous enemies. At this moment, all there is to go on is a skimpy cop report and the hospital spokeswoman's statement that he sustained a serious head injury and is in a comatose state."

"You mean the report saying it's characteristic of the driver falling asleep since there weren't any skid marks. The bright side is at least the cops are continuing their investigation at county impound where the vehicle was towed."

Jeannette's brow raised slightly as if in doubt of the facts. "And what's your opinion?"

"I discussed it with Tucker and we both agree it sounds pretty suspicious. Maybe it's like in the movies where someone cuts the brake line or sabotages the steering wheel," I said somewhat jokingly.

My attempt at humor didn't even produce a grin.

"So you think his accident could be linked to attempted murder?" She said it with such an earnest expression I felt a little ridiculous having compared the gravity of the situation to a movie plot. "Until the

25

investigation is wrapped up, we'll play the accident as a fairly significant event because of his standing in the community, whether liked or disliked. And since the only known witness is unable to say anything yet, it'll have to focus mainly on his background. Maybe that will produce a reaction that'll be useful. It might flush out some of the riffraff from his past who felt it was time he was out of the picture."

She got up from the desk and I watched her backside move toward Rusty Gates' office. "Got anyone in mind?" I said as a parting question.

She did a one-eighty, pivoting on the high heel of her cowboy boot, her skirt flaring out and her long sandy brown hair floating along with the swirl. "Didn't he and that Las Vegas developer have a tussle?"

Unfortunately, I wasn't able to do much of a follow-up on the Saville vs. Banyan bout. Saville had left town, and as for Banyan, after plunging his car off an embankment and rolling it several times, he wasn't in any condition to comment. So, I contacted Banyan's wife, Blanche, who ran the Red River Coalition, a conservation group founded by the couple.

She invited me out to their thousand-acre ranch, and from within the confines of Banyan's compound, she provided a description of Derrick Banyan's condition, which hadn't altered much from the initial deep-sleep state he'd been in since the accident.

"When I stood at his bedside, Derrick seemed at peace, even though horribly battered. Just like his spirit when faced with adversity. His presence never felt stronger, as if Derrick's mission in life is too precious to abandon. He's a survivor, you know?"

"I can only imagine," I said.

Following that, she centered on other concerns Banyan had been facing. "He would insist we focus on opposing the Sorrow Creek project and moving forward on all his other goals and aspirations regarding the environmental degradation of our planet. And most importantly, not dwell on the weakened state he lies in now. In other words, beyond what is out of our control." Blanche's matter-of-fact stance quickly turned into a sanguine tone, "We feel lost without him and hope for a quick recovery."

I quoted her verbatim, but it was material that didn't work easily into a story about a local radical, possibly on the verge of death after brawling with a Las Vegas developer. So, I concentrated on getting Saville's reaction.

Vegas Vic wasn't listed in the phone directory at Nevada Resorts International headquarters, but an operator said he was traveling and his number confidential. She took a message and hung up, making me feel even more disconnected than I did after Blanche Banyan's statement.

I took the hint and temporarily gave up on trying to make more out of Derrick Banyan's car wreck than the official police statements. Saville would eventually return to Great Valley and I'd be there to greet him.

Meanwhile I focused on Banyan's history for the upcoming feature story Jeannette wanted. The piece backpedaled a bit, mostly describing Banyan as one of the new western breed of environmentally conscious ranchers instead of an eco-warrior injured after fighting a proposed lakefront leisure community under the guise of siphoning off water to Las Vegas:

Banyan's Life Hangs In Balance After Jeep Accident

Derrick Banyan remains in a coma at Alden Memorial Hospital in Crescent City after his vehicle rolled two nights ago. Banyan's wife, Blanche Banyan, says the coalition will remain vigilant over his environmental concerns until he is able to make a full recovery.

On the surface Derrick Banyan might seem like a simple rancher dedicated to improving the old way of ranching. But he had his detractors as well as his admirers.

Since the inception of his Red River Coalition, consisting mostly of environmental activists like himself, Banyan has been labeled a radical revolutionary.

His 1,000-acre ranch consists of various conservation projects in advanced irrigation, organic meat cultivation and holistic crop methods. Because of this arrangement, Banyan has been the recipient of several agricultural subsidies, which has drawn criticism from area farmers and ranchers. There are strong sentiments he is receiving government handouts

28

for nothing but window dressing on projects other ranchers have been involved with all along, in some form or another, without all of the taxpayer incentives.

Blanche Banyan said Derrick took it all in stride. "If he hadn't brought a lot of these issues to the forefront, we'd still be overgrazing our national forests and polluting our natural resources like there's no tomorrow."

However, she had admitted the topping on the federal dole are his fish ponds filled with the only endangered razorback chubs left in the west. Since they are a desirable species to several wildlife agencies, Derrick Banyan had been well compensated for the suckers.

He had rarely been seen puttering around the ranch though. As a conservationist, he had spent most of his time involved in fund-raising, lobbying and recruiting members for various causes around the country. And, like the ranks of others with such distinction, he had frequently been the topic of news articles describing his deeds as an activist, usually doing battle with heavyweights such as Omni Oil Corporation and Wyoming Coal.

Jeannette insisted on a follow-up the next day. "Wily, it's obvious Banyan knew how to milk the bureaucratic cow on his miles of prime real estate along the Red River," she said. "You'd think the only thing lacking in his life was some kind of justice served on various corporations for their atrocities to the environment. And I would say specifically, Omni's oil shale projects. Go get 'em tiger." She laughed, averting her eyes from my apparent amusement at her statement. Her computer screen served as a good diversion while she acted like work was her main focus.

But I wasn't going to let her get away so easily. To draw her attention I said, "What's that supposed to mean?"

"Look, I think you're catching on is all. You've been here more than a week and you've developed that carnivorous attitude Rusty is looking for in a reporter."

"If I didn't know any better I'd say you enjoyed that."

Jeannette smiled at my attempt to reestablish eye contact, then looked up from her screen at me. "In your dreams. Now, Wily Spiver, I've got work to concentrate on instead of some kind of flirtation or pass you're imagining. If you want to engage a woman in conversation try Blanche Banyan again." She seemed so business-like that I let it drop, pretense and all, and within fifteen minutes the only thing on my mind was the drive out to Banyan's ranch.

It was by luck that Blanche was home. She had been spending most of her time at the hospital, she told me. I wasn't sure I believed her for some reason. I guess it was the way she never seemed rushed or harried, just short and rude.

The second interview with Blanche Banyan developed into a feature story on her husband's constant battle against river erosion. "Derrick has worked extensively with the Corps of Engineers as part of a government program to protect riparian areas while restoring our farmland." And then instead of talking about riverbanks reinforced with logs and timbers, Blanche Banyan got off on a tirade about Omni polluting the river with a variety of contaminates from their oil shale operation.

I pushed the issue as to whether she thought her husband put himself in danger by fighting local traditions, to the point of receiving death threats.

"Although we lost that battle to a corrupt federal magistrate, there was no way Omni could escape the bad publicity it generated." Blanche smiled slightly at her husband's accomplishment. "I don't think he ever took any kind of threat personally."

We were ensconced on the front porch of their palatial log-cabin lodge under a warm afternoon sun. I was comfortably reclined in an Adirondack chair, while Blanche Banyan anxiously paced back and forth in cowboy boots that thudded on the wooden planks. While she was engrossed in talking about their latest foe at hand, I was absorbed in the peaceful backdrop of the Bookcliffs palisade stretching above undulating fields of green alfalfa.

She interrupted my reverie by saying, "Stop them now or they'll own everything sacred, including the damn rain."

It was obvious she was vehemently opposed to corporate acquisition, or put on a convincing act. I'd always been skeptical of over the top statements and people who dressed like they were on stage. But

Blanche? She was dressed like an Australian outback hunter in her floppy canvas hat, plaid shirt and blue jeans. The getup looked authentic, like she belonged in the wild as much as the tall leafy cottonwoods lining their drive, so I had no reason to doubt her sincerity.

"You feel threatened?" I said, and looked down another gravel drive of this 'modest' homestead to where horses stood listlessly in the corrals. A two-story barn the size of an airplane hanger adjoined the corrals.

"All the time." Blanche Banyan was also gazing, but more at the inward reflection on what she'd said. "Faster than a spinning drill bit, they are gaining footholds in every facet of our lives. And I'm not sure I want any part of it."

"I mean threatened like you might be in some kind of danger," I said. "Like maybe Derrick's crash wasn't an accident?"

She stared intensely at me. "If you think so, let me in on what you find out." With that she concluded the interview with: "Now if you'll excuse me, I've got work to do."

Of course no excuses were ever necessary. I'd heard it all before. I thought, sure, Ms. Banyan, anything you say. I'm just here to make sure we have a working relationship from now on. What would she say to that?

She just shot me a glance. "Nice you could take the time to come all this way. Wily, is it? I'll be anxious to see what you've written. Please be kind. Lately the stress has been killing me, with my husband's health and all." She smiled, glancing at her watch. We stood in unison and she shook my hand loosely, as a form of servant dismissal, before I had a chance to ask her about her husband's condition.

3

By the time I got back to the office and filed my story everyone had gone for the day, so I headed home. As I approached the lobby, I could hear Lucy's voice echoing off the walls. Listening to her sing usually lightened my mood. After all, her effervescent personality was contagious as well. Despite the dregs of motel life, she managed to accept her position with a degree of indifference. Or not – since it might not have mattered if she planned on leaving anyway in pursuit of a singing career.

"I got to get out of this place . . . if it's the last thing I ever doooo." She crooned to an old song that played through speakers in the lobby's ceiling, then she went into the back office and turned down the music. When she reappeared she told me that it really was time to get away from this place. "I'm on the verge of starting a singing career. What do you think?"

"Great. You sing like you mean it," I said. There was a raw, raspy fervor rising from her vocal cords.

She could have passed as a young Stevie Nicks impersonator in Vegas.

"My dream is to be lead singer for a band out in Cal. There's no group worth hooking up with around here. So it's California here I come, baby," she said, then frowned. "You know, though, I'll probably never get out of this damn dump."

Earlier on she had asked me what the odds were of her getting a job singing in some lounge act in Vegas. I didn't know, honestly. My father had worked for casinos; I was always on the other side of the tables. "But you're from Vegas," she had pleaded. "You must know someone in the entertainment business."

"Yeah, cocktail waitresses and strippers, or as they are also referred to, nude models. I used to work for a smut magazine. There's always a good chance you could work as a model. I know the publisher, Rudy Morris. With a body like yours all you gotta do is smile for the camera. It's easy. Just take off all your clothes and you're hired."

"That's not for me," she had said.

"It wasn't for me either, and I was just the copywriter not a nude model. Even after a couple of years you really never get used to the business." I hadn't told her the part about paychecks feeding my gambling habit. And besides, Morris was a nice enough guy, kinda like a father figure to all his help.

She said she'd pass. I couldn't blame her. Lucy didn't need to take that route. Her voice could carry her away, along with her listeners, to a better place. I hoped anyway.

I walked over to the icemaker, grabbed a bucket on top of the machine for the drink I thought I needed.

Eloy Munn, Lucy's stepfather and owner of the Lucky U Motel, liked the ice where it could be watched, since a common practice among guests was to unload all of the watery cubes from the machine into coolers before heading down the road.

"Hey, Lucy," I said over the thud of ice dropping into the small plastic bucket, "Want to take a break and have a drink at my place?" She lit **NO** on the vacancy sign and we went upstairs to my room.

At first she sat at the round table while I poured drinks. For a motel room it was spacious enough to have a queen size bed with night stand and dresser. There was a kitchenette off to one side with a mini-fridge and a small RV sized stove built into a counter with a sink. Alongside the counter was a table with two chairs.

When I handed her the drink she went to the bed, moved a pillow over and sat down with her back resting against the headboard.

"Those cheap chairs really suck," she said.

I agreed, sitting on the end of the bed. "I was hoping to get more comfortable."

"Pretty convenient having a bed in the living room." She slipped out of her shoes and extended her legs to where her feet touched my thigh. Then poked me with her big toe and said, "Don't you think?"

"That's because of the nice room you gave me."

"Sweet, isn't it? And it's even got a radio."

We listened to the radio, while lying and playing on the bed, swigging whiskey and 7-Up, and got completely liberated of all our material things and inhibitions. Afterward I felt relaxed and uninhibited, free from any type of constraint.

Lucy suggested we watch a movie. She had access to the motel's VCR machine that piped videotape into all the rooms. Free movies weren't advertised on the marquee. It was illegal as hell. But Eloy Munn did it anyway as a way to keep his preferred clientele, mostly hunters, traveling salesmen, and those who came to visit their loved ones in the prison camp a few miles away, happy as clams.

"Wanna watch *Repo Man*?" Lucy asked.

"Sure, why not?" We hustled back down the stairs to the lobby's small back office, where a large collection of videos lined the walls.

"Got to *love* Emilio," she said. "He's so cool. You know he's the brother of Charlie Sheen?"

"Yeah. Martin Sheen's son. Ever see *Apocalypse Now*?" I asked, focusing on Lucy's lovely breasts as she stooped down to retrieve the movie from the lower shelf in the cramped, cluttered office.

"No. I don't like war movies. Way too much blood and guts, I guess. Saw *Platoon* though. Charlie was in that one. I went to see it because of him."

She plugged the tape into the machine, hit the play button and led me out of the office, through the lobby, up the stairs and down the hall.

"You know," I said, as we walked down the narrow passageway, "Emilio also played in a Stephen King movie called *Maximum Overdrive*, where he fights semi-trucks out to commit genocide because they are under the influence of a rogue comet."

37

"Cool. The guy's got style. Kinda like you, Wily, battling rogue influences." She laughed loudly enough to wake the neighbors, then stumbled into the room. It was only after I opened the door and flopped on the bed that I realized she might be right about fighting off demons.

Crazy as it was, halfway through *Repo Man* I started having a panic attack, maybe caused by the bizarre twist the movie was taking, or all the alcohol. So, I told Lucy I had to sleep or I would be too tired and hung over the next day. She wasn't all that happy about it, because it reminded her that she was shirking the front desk duties. "Don't be a stranger, stop by more often," she said, then left. I fell into a nightmare about a giant black chopper hovering over me with a menacing hook swinging around my head.

The next day, I arrived early at the large mercantile building that had been converted into the *Beacon*'s office. Instead of dry goods, there were computers everywhere. The old brick building had been hollowed out to hold the paper's central nervous system, with fabric wall dividers separating various departments. Along with other editorial detritus was my desk, it had a little yellow message pasted to the computer screen saying that Chief Higgins had returned my call with specifics about the Banyan vs. Saville fight.

With the phone cradled between ear and shoulder, I dialed his number then hunched over the keyboard. After salutations he began with the police report and I began typing: "A patrol unit had cruised by the Lucky U Motel and saw the suspects arguing in the parking lot. Before it escalated into a full-blown assault, Sanchez intervened," said Higgins. "Officer Sanchez noticed Saville had a gun at the time, but Saville has a concealed carry permit issued by the Las Vegas PD. He was warned about the need to acquire another permit here if he planned to stay for an extended period. In the meanwhile, he's registered it with our office. I'm telling you this, Spiver, since it's part of the report. But I'd rather you not make a big deal of it since he didn't draw on Banyan as far we could tell."

I compiled my notes into a story, and considered concealing the firearm bit, then decided against it. I concluded the piece with: "Saville was armed at the time of the incident, but was not cited due to the fact he has a permit to carry a concealed weapon."

The waning afternoon sun in the big plate glass windows of a bygone storefront made the office a stifling inferno. The hot air started to lull me to sleep. There was a need to move about before I became completely comatose. I decided it was time to visit the Clerk and Recorder at the old brownstone county courthouse and do research on Sorrow Creek Basin property rights.

"It's a mess out there, with what the oil and gas companies own and the ranchers don't. Some of them have mineral rights, others have leases, or they own 'em outright. But Omni must've got a hold of a lot of the senior holdings when they leased most of the BLM tracts up top the Bookcliffs," said Margie Leveta, head clerk. I had heard from Jeannette that she had been working in the office since high school; she now looked to be in her late thirties. She knew a lot, but still had a rough time with pinpointing who owned what in the Sorrow Creek Basin "You know,

39

I know almost every rancher in the county," she said, then walked back along a row of shelves while I waited at the counter. "But with all of the oil companies claims, deeds and mineral rights becoming part of the county picture, it's so muddied and complex no one has been able to figure it out except for the company lawyers. And they're always willing to interpret what you're looking at."

After I left the Clerk and Recorder, my hopes were raised when I ran into Victor Saville leaving the commissioners' office. He reminded me of the many casino bosses my father associated with when I was growing up in Las Vegas. He was tall, dark and heavy set with greased back hair, dressed in the trademark dark pinstriped suit. There was more to Slick Vic than his hair, though. Saville was a covert kind of guy who was probably well connected, someone you didn't fuck with. We both gave an acknowledging glance at each other.

"Just the man I wanted to see," I announced, even though Saville didn't look like he wanted to see me. "How's Vegas these days, Vic? Does the forecast call for long term drought or wet climate?"

"That supposed to be funny?" He looked puzzled, then frowned, his stare interrogating.

"I'm the guy across the hall, Wily Spiver. Remember me?"

"Yeah, I know. I usually never forget a face, especially a wise-ass reporter, Wily Spiver. I know a Spiver out of Vegas. Any relation?" His eyes drifted down, sizing me up.

"Doubt it."

"Sure? You look familiar, like there's a resemblance to someone or something."

"Yep, I'm sure." I'd never met Saville prior to the commissioners' meeting or heard talk of him. It was possible he knew of my family, but my father always liked keeping family and work separate.

"So okay then," he said. "Things are rolling right along with Sorrow Creek. We're hopeful the commissioners will give us a green light soon. But nothing's official. Guess you can toss that into that scrap book of yours."

"Thank you. And any comment on the incident about a week ago at the Lucky U?"

"I'm not following." The beady stare returned.

"The fight between you and Derrick Banyan ring a bell? It's official news now. You two made the cop blotter for disturbing the peace at the motel. How's that possible?"

There was no quoting Saville on the fight at the motel. He insisted all that misunderstanding had been cleared up with the cops and Banyan. "Look, I know it's your job, but save the inquiring mind for when the questions amount to something besides a libel suit against your paper," he said, adding, "With a little cooperation, you'll get an exclusive on the Sorrow Creek deal when it's approved." Then he turned and walked away, the soles of his shoes echoing off the marble hallway.

After the temporary setback, I tried to see any of the three commissioners, but a surly secretary in the empty confines of the reception room said they were in meetings all afternoon. Obviously, I wasn't accepted into the bureaucratic society. On the other hand, if I were that pretty young blonde from the

41

Crescent City News, Sally Sawmaker, I'd have a VIP pass. She was the major competition for the *Beacon*. During the interview with Rusty Gates and Jeannette LeBreeze, Gates had told me about her; that she was extremely competitive, thorough in her reporting, very attractive and had all the right connections. With her ambitions she'd go far as a journalist. "So what I'm telling you is watch out, she's a real pro. I can tell by your clips that you're not bad either, so I expect great shit from you," he said.

Oh, sure, I'm your guy, I thought. Just give me a big fat raise. Or at least what I made writing for the porn magazine I used to work for in Vegas. But I told him, "Of course. It's part of the job description, isn't it?"

Money wasn't the main issue anyway. I had to leave Vegas regardless of how little I made. I had a gambling problem, and no matter how much I earned it wasn't enough to feed the addiction. The newspaper clippings I had given Gates were from the last job I had in St. George, Utah. It had paid even less than he was giving me.

4

I headed back to the office where time passed uncomfortably slowly. For starters, there was a noticeable lack of oxygen. Everything moved at a lethargic pace yet with a sense of urgency, like gasping for air after being underwater too long. Ad reps and production staff hustled between the department cubicles in a frenzied state, consulting one another concerning ad copy for tomorrow's run. I worked the phones until there wasn't anyone on the other end with anything to say. That is until six-thirty when Ms. Banyan returned my call. She was pissed.

She said, "Victor Saville is nothing more than a sleazy developer who is as reckless as Omni Oil for leasing its water rights for a storage dam in a semi-dry river basin."

Blanche Banyan was giving me one of those moments of inspiration, a splinter of hope for some juicy quotes, until I pushed her on the offhanded chance Victor Saville might have had something to do with Banyan's accident. "Why would you think that?"

"Don't you think that it's highly unlikely your husband would fall asleep less than a mile from your home?"

"Who said anything about sleep?"

"Or mechanical failure of any sort since he was probably going less than forty?" I said.

"You know," she said, "anything is possible. They say it could've been a blowout. And I haven't heard anything to suggest foul play. Higgins also told me the flat tire could have been caused by a delineator post after it was hit."

"So far the police think it's an accident and there's really no evidence to make me think otherwise."

There was a long pause, followed by, "I can't comment any further without consulting the coalition's board of trustees," making it clear that any quote about the fight was off limits. "But I will say off the record, Saville's a fucking prick. That's all there is to it. However, I don't like resorting to tabloid journalism. Why don't we let it go at that," she said, then abruptly gave me a goodbye.

When I started wrapping everything up for the night, Jeannette LeBreeze strolled over to see what was happening. "How's tomorrow's cover story look?" she said, sitting in the hard-backed chair next to my desk.

"If it had wings, it might fly." It was a bit optimistic on my part and she seemed to sense it, so I added, "Banyan's brawl with Saville is definitely worth pursuing, but it's going to be hard to get his side of the story since he's in a coma."

"So you're winging it, is that what you mean?" she said, then suggested grabbing a bite. After getting a good look at her dazzling baby blues, I agreed. Although we had become friendlier over the last couple of weeks, this was the first time she had offered to do anything together outside of the office setting.

"I've had about enough of this for the day, and Blanche isn't in a talkative mood. She's hinted at things, like threats on his life, but won't say anything definitive or quotable."

"She probably thinks you're the pushy type. You know, not happy until you get what you want."

"That's what *you* think, but I'm not really. I just think there's something that doesn't jive with the scenario and I'm trying to get to the root of it. Besides, it makes the job so much more fun, I mean worthwhile, like solving a puzzle." I shot Jen a smile to show that I was joking.

She frowned in return and said, "Would you please not fret about it tonight? You'll have a few more hours tomorrow before deadline to sort it all out. Remember, that's eleven sharp to you. Maybe she'll loosen up by morning. I'm getting hungry. Do you plan on working all night?"

"Not at all. Let's go eat," I said, although with some degree of skepticism. I tend to stay out of people's personal lives unless the job required it. "If I'm not mistaken, don't you have a husband at home waiting for you?"

"Away on a so-called business trip. Besides, doesn't matter, we're separated."

"If he won't object, then I'll not keep the lady waiting."

"Save the theatrics, he doesn't care. But if you're going to agonize over an unfinished story at dinner, I'd rather wait until you're finished."

"We're out of here shortly," I said, feeling somewhat under duress without at least a story outline regarding Banyan's connection to the Sorrow Creek project and the fight with Saville. Derrick Banyan obviously had a plan of attack against Saville's project besides the hallway incident. "I just need another half hour to polish off a story idea."

The rough draft took off on an angle based mostly on speculation, which placed Derrick Banyan center stage with his past performance before the commissioners and Saville's group. The story angle assumed The Red River Coalition would block the project with lawsuits, even if Banyan was in a coma. I wrapped it up with a graphic account of the motel fight that I hoped would be incorporated in the final copy, despite Saville's admission that it was only a misunderstanding between he and Banyan. I saved it to a memory stick as backup, then sent the original over to Jeannette, who looked ready to leave at any minute.

"I think you'll find this entertaining. It was the best I could do given the situation. So were you about to leave without me?"

She ignored the question by asking her own: "What situation?"

"I've given you a rough outline of what could make tomorrow's headline. I elaborated some since no one's talking much about the Saville and Banyan confrontation. I'm hoping the chief will fill in some of the details from the police report and Blanche is willing to cooperate in the morning."

She read it with some amusement. "So this is it? I'm laughing, you know. Rusty might like it though, if it's all factual." She scowled in mock fashion at me from her computer screen. "You finally ready?"

It was another warm spring evening so we walked the few blocks from the office to Pitt's Barbecue Barn. It was catfish for me and a steak for Jen. I ordered a beer while she had a glass of house Chablis. At first talk centered mostly on Rusty Gates and the financial problems the paper was experiencing.

Even though I was a newcomer with few insights into the financial working of the *Great Valley Beacon*, that didn't stop me from asking Jen how the paper was doing. I had assumed things were fine, considering its size. The staff consisted of three sales reps, two full time production people, a receptionist, and four editorial members, plus several freelance writers and stringers. And it had the right ratio of ads to copy to be making a profit.

"You mean, is he stealing the business blind? In a sense, yes." She said it as a matter of fact and stared at me with a somber expression. "From what I can see, he's probably using the revenue to pay his gambling debts."

Another one of those, I thought, a person with similar interests. "Oh yeah. I didn't know that. Do you think the paper will fold?"

"There are always buyers for a paper that is in the county seat of record." Jeannette nibbled away at a cheese stick appetizer, and without missing a bite, said, "He's managed to cook the books so it looks like a rosy scenario instead of a bed of thorns."

47

I tried to look at the bright side. "Even if the paper might be in financial straits, everyone is still getting paid, right?"

"For now. But how long, I've got no idea. I can't just move on like you when the job runs out though. I need a steady paycheck. My husband and I are talking divorce."

"Sorry to hear that. I hope it's amicable." That was all I could say. She had taken me by surprise with things I wasn't sure I wanted to know at that point. "Someone'll buy it if Rusty sells out."

"Like the competition? Then what? The *Crescent City News* already has a full time staff, or what's left of it. With the downfall of newspapers around the country there seems to be a glut of editors looking for work."

"You're a talented woman. I'm sure something will come along," I said, to fill the gap that was starting to come between us. Then I tried levity to change the subject. "Let's run away together. Just kidding, of course." I didn't know where that came from, maybe wanting to get a rise out of her, or it just came naturally. After all, she was an attractive woman in her early thirties without any excess baggage besides a current husband.

She rolled her eyes at that comment. "Ha, ha. You couldn't afford me."

"Anything is possible with the right combination."

"What's that supposed to mean?"

"Rusty isn't the only one who likes putting everything on the line," I said.

"Gee, you're a gambler too? Never would have guessed," she said sarcastically. "I can't believe I'm listening to someone who thinks the road to riches leads to a slot machine." She then feigned amazement with: "But how else would we survive on a meager reporter's salary?"

"Faith or fate, take your pick. But from past experiences, there's more of a chance at collecting thirty grand in a week than working a year for the paper." She was frowning again so I quickly added: "That's not entirely true, but I like to joke about it anyway. Rest assured, I breathe a lot easier outside a casino."

"So how's your breathing now?"

"Like I got the wind knocked out of me. Is this conversation really happening between us?"

She flashed me a smile and glanced around the dining room at tables and booths, empty when we arrived, but now occupied with recognizable people from around town. I wondered who was eavesdropping, though most patrons talked among themselves and seemed oblivious to us.

Since Jeannette was only contemplating divorce and still technically married, it wasn't any picnic and suddenly seemed questionable to be seen eating with her in a restaurant where I felt as visible to everyone as the pies and cakes in the six-foot dessert carrousel that twirled around at the front door old-fashioned style.

"Why don't we go to my place?" I wanted to escape public scrutiny. I felt vulnerable, as if someone could cut a slice out of my life just by misreading the situation and passing it along. Although, we were deceiving ourselves if we thought we were just having a business meeting over dinner. And then there was my new friend, Lucy, who I really liked – we were just friends though. One date doesn't make for a commitment or long term relationship. Some might see it differently, so I pushed that thought aside and tried to focus on the present.

"Can't. I still have a husband someplace. You know, we wouldn't be sitting here if . . ." She trailed off in quiet contemplation, in the awkwardness of potentially cheating on someone she probably still loved to a degree.

I interrupted her thought process with, "I agree that we should stick to business from now on."

"Knock it off." She said. There was a slight quiver to her voice and a wrinkle to her brow.

"I was being positive. I'd like to think of us as friends, not lovers." I was starting to think the best parts of our conversation were deteriorating into the abyss of us committing adultery. It was a world beginning to look dark and foreboding, a place almost too scary to enter. It was hell as sure as there are hedonistic virgins and pagan Christians. It wasn't right, and yet it felt natural at the time.

"I thought you were a trustworthy guy, Wily Spiver. Now, all I think you want is a quick lay because you're a horny bastard." To be sure, she had slid out of her low-heeled shoe and put a foot in my crotch for a random inspection under the tablecloth. "What'd I tell you?" She quickly removed her foot before it became apparent to anyone what her intentions were.

I couldn't believe how this heavy flirtation was affecting me; that she was coming on to me so aggressively. It was hard to contain my emotions. "I'm really not ready for this. And after all, you're my boss. Let's wait and see what happens after you get a divorce," I said, almost apologetically because I couldn't keep my eyes off her. She was a stunning woman in her white blouse and knee high skirt.

"Sorry. I was just thinking it could be a long dry spell for me. We're off to see our marriage counselor or a lawyer in a few days. That *could* change my disposition."

"But didn't you just indicate . . ."

"Sorry, Wily. I still have to try and make things work out."

"Good, and that's the way it should be. This has all become way too twisted if you think I'm here just to get screwed," I said matter-of-factly, after feeling somewhat let down.

"That'd be the therapy I really need, but my husband insists on taking the conventional route," she said, slightly amused by the idea. "Just humoring you. Don't look so serious. I haven't cheated on my husband."

"That's a relief. I was beginning to think we were starting to step over the line."

"Nonsense. I like you, Wily. There's a bit of an imp in you I find healthy. You're truthful, somewhat shy, but with a sense of humor I find appealing. I'm sure you've been around a bit in your wanderings, that you're not stuck in some rut or want any kind of a permanent relationship, like the guy I married ten years ago."

Whatever that meant, I didn't particularly want to know. My thoughts wallowed on such things as moral depravity. In the scheme of things it seemed good and bad worked together like Yin and Yang. But were we being led to hell or delivered from evil?

Where I grew up, debauchery was a way of life you learned to accept as the nature of things, no matter what side of the Yin and Yang fence you were on. Anyone in denial was a hypocrite. But that was the paradoxical way of Las Vegas. And I just assumed it applied everywhere light casts a shadow.

After wishing Jen good night, I headed toward the office, following Progress Avenue through the darkness below a burned out streetlight. Dazed and addled by the mix of beer and melodramatic moments at Pitt's BBQ Barn, I looked for a light at the end of the tunnel, but only saw the neon sign for the Portal Bar.

The Portal sounded good. I walked in, sat at the bar and ordered a draw beer. I plugged the jukebox and played an oldie I was surprised to see listed. People had been strung up in redneck joints like the Portal for what the song implied. Then again, with a room full of barroom philosophers with a song about a transvestite in a mixed up, shook up world was as appropriate as any. After all, bigotry and prejudice was an atmosphere some of the regulars seemed to enjoy from time to time, judging by their chosen vocabulary.

Raw music emerged full blast from the speakers, asking the question why she acts like a woman and talks like a man. I thought, what the hell, it could happen to anyone who was discontented with the way things turned out. Although the Kinks were putting a nice spin on it, I didn't need to role play to understand life alone could be a drag at times. But finding salvation as a transvestite wasn't my style.

My fashionable wardrobe consisted of jeans, a few Oxford dress shirts and tennis shoes for running around to a variety of municipal buildings and offices. Or sometimes slacks to go with the khaki look for those special occasions like Chamber banquets. Loafers were also acceptable footwear, or a pair of hiking boots with steel toes (for those social activities at a bar when I might get stepped on or needed to kick something).

Besides, what did style have to do with anything, anyway? What could've possibly been said that wouldn't sound gauche? I had simply learned to accept what was dished out in life by the places I frequented. I'd become accustomed to the shrimp cocktails and surf and turf menus at some of the casinos in Vegas. Now, two-thirds of my intake came from takeout. Give me a cheeseburger with fries any day of the week, or a couple of smothered burritos with shredded lettuce and tomatoes, and I'd feel my daily nutritional requirements were met.

"Want another?" asked Red, the bartender.

"Why not?" I said while glancing in the mirror at Jim Tucker walking through the door. "How about making it two of the same, Red?"

I waved Tucker over. He was dressed to the hilt for the Portal, with a tie and sport coat. "What's with the look?" I asked right off.

"A Chamber of Commerce mix. The pro-gambling group was celebrating their victory to put the gaming initiative on the ballot for the upcoming election."

"Anyone in the group named Victor Saville?"

"Of course. He and a bunch of local yokel businessmen. One of the sponsors hosted the open

53

house at his real estate office. Couldn't miss that one. Rusty's been riding me to do stories on the major backers and what their contributions amount to. He also wanted to confirm who the mayor's political ties are. You know, as popular as gaming has become for these little depression spots on the state map, it might be prime time for Great Valley to be a part of it."

Tucker was right about casino towns sprouting up all over the place. There were three old mining towns which had been converted into gambling havens with loads of money. They were towns on the verge of turning into ghosts, and all within a day's drive of Great Valley.

Now I was curious how far it went. "Any mention of Saville's development being included?"

"Not directly, since it's outside town limits, but you can bet casinos to donuts if voters are money hungry enough, gambling halls and hookers will be as much a part of the landscape as a lake and golf course when that resort community becomes annexed."

"Naturally."

"Wouldn't that be right up your alley, Spiver. Didn't you work for some adult entertainment magazine in Vegas?"

"Yeah, and I've always thought that was a career lowlight," I said honestly.

"What's so special about working for the *Beacon*?"

"I'm thinking tonight that, like the name, it's been a guiding light for finding myself in the company of the ideal woman."

"What the *hell* are you talking about?" he demanded.

54

"Not what but whom. Like Jen, for instance."

"Ooh, hold on there, partner. I'm not some barroom drunkard who needs a story like that to be kept entertained. She's married to a guy who probably doesn't believe in damage control," he said with a straight face to my reflection behind the bar.

"Separated. Anyway, sorry. It just sort of slipped out." I starred back in the glass with a lot of respect for Jim Tucker, and hadn't wanted to drag him into my fate. Happily married men don't want to hear it, and rightfully so. And I didn't like saying anything, but he was the only one I could confide in who might have understood the dynamics of the situation.

"Look, Spiver, she's a dynamite gal. Great looking, sharp mind and all, but she's pretty hard-boiled and, I would think, looking for more than a good time in a cheap motel. Or think of it this way, you could get hurt, if not physically then emotionally. Even if she thinks a divorce is the way out, I doubt she's serious."

"What makes you say that?"

"For starters, he makes too much money. And they don't live in a motel."

"Yeah, yeah. I know, you're right. I need to drop that thought and pursue other opportunities." And I wanted to change the subject before I also had to face the guilty party in the mirror.

"I thought you and Lucy over at the motel were hitting it off." Tucker knew her. She was a friend of his wife's. "She's someone you can trust. Straightforward and not pretentious. A real catch."

"A great gal, I know. It's just that Jeannette threw me a curve ball tonight and I swung at it thinking it was a home run or something. They're both nice gals."

Tucker ignored the comment. He had a wary countenance in the mirror before saying, "Speaking of dynamic women. You wouldn't believe who was at the chamber party yakking it up with the commissioners. Blanche Banyan."

"You're right. I don't believe it. Unless she was there to trash the party instead of crashing it." I said it sarcastically.

"I got the impression she was getting the VIP treatment for whatever reason. Maybe everyone was feeling sympathetic about her husband being in a coma."

There seemed to be more than just irony about her attending a chamber function. "Doesn't that seem like a contradiction? Derrick wouldn't have anything to do with gambling or the commissioners and yet here she is schmoozing with the dignitaries. Seems odd is all." Jim Tucker never did give me an answer, but I didn't need him to tell me something didn't mix well with that scenario. It would be an angle to pursue.

5

I made deadline at eleven sharp the next morning without a single quote from Blanche Banyan. The front page story was a follow-up to Banyan's accident and included the police report about the fight at the motel.

Sometimes there's a fine line whether to include negative aspects in a story about a victim of his own circumstance. But it's also hard to ignore facts involving an altercation between Banyan and Saville that's released in a police blotter and might be relevant in some way. Whatever the case, one thing I was sure to be careful of was not to extract anything from last night's rough draft that wasn't part of the initial cop report.

Sure enough, Chief Higgins called after that day's edition hit the streets and wanted me to pay him a visit. I was buzzed through the security doors, and then escorted to the chief's office by dispatcher Rita.

Under the grayish hue of fluorescent lighting, Tom Higgins sat staring at his computer screen. I pulled up the seat opposite, a hard, plastic molded chair matching the office's achromatic color scheme. Everything in the room was a shade of gray, including his mood.

Higgins tapped away with his middle finger on the keyboard. It looked like he was scrolling files. We briefly exchanged greetings in this clinical setting with its antiseptic aura.

"What's up?" I finally asked Higgins, who continued to fool on the keyboard with a sort of protracted disinterest in my presence.

"I was wondering that myself." He pushed the keyboard aside and fiddled with a pencil, which he rolled between his thumb and fingers. "You have intentionally led some of your readers to think there was more to the accident than our preliminary investigation turned up." The pencil stalled and he looked sharply at me.

"I just reminded readers that Banyan was involved in a fight with Victor Saville the night before the accident at the Lucky U. And the exact cause of the rollover crash is still in doubt," I said, sitting stone-faced sober, staring back at Higgins. When visiting with the chief, I felt like a suspect about to go under the surgical knife of interrogation. He ignored my response by looking down at the newspaper on his desk. Below the headline was a picture of the crash site where deputies sifted through debris.

"Those incidents are totally unrelated. In your story it suggests Saville might have something to do with the accident. That's the way I read it and possibly others as well. I think you reporter types use the term yellow journalism to describe it. Someone who exploits, distorts or exaggerates the news in order to create a sensation and attract readers. I looked it up and wanted to make it clear you understand it too. The other reason I called was to update Banyan's situation," he said without expression or emotion.

"I hope it's positive. And that nobody wanted to threaten his life," I said, but didn't apologize for the way I'd written the story. It was objective, factual, and despite the chief's editorial comments favoring omissions, it wasn't slanted.

"Who do you think wants him dead?" The chief eyed me skeptically, staring at my reporter notebook and pen as if they were potential weapons.

"I thought he had a few enemies around here, that's all. Victor Saville being one of them, considering their attitude toward each other over the Sorrow Creek deal."

"Maybe, but Banyan's never reported any death threats. The wreckage hasn't revealed anything specific because of the extensive damage, but the state's crime scene unit is still looking into it. Anyway, Banyan is expected to pull through, eventually. The doctors say he's showing some signs of life. So you can tell your readers we'll have more information when he recovers enough to discuss anything pertinent to our investigation."

"Have a timeline?" I asked.

"The doc wasn't too specific, only that he's responding to stimuli the nurses have provided over the last couple of days." The chief had been observing me write everything down, and added, "And you can quote me on that."

The trivial remark made us both smile a bit, relieving the escalating tension. But I wanted more out of this meeting than to be glad-handed. I asked him if he thought Banyan was the target of a murder plot. "The vehicle is so badly damaged a cursory inspection shows nothing unusual. That's about it for now."

I thanked him generously for the update. Although it wasn't much, he did say he'd have answers eventually, and I quoted him on that, for what it was worth.

Instead of relying on a lack of information, I decided to visit Banyan in the big city, hoping the nurses would allow me into the intensive care unit.

It was an hour's drive west to Crescent City, and into a sunset with spectacular arrays of red and orange that fused with the surrounding sandstone cliffs and hills, making it hard to differentiate earth from sky. Wispy clouds formed patterns weaved with the curving rock formations of the Bookcliffs.

I arrived in Crescent City within the allotted visiting hours of the ICU. All that was left of the sunset was a fading gray-blue sky on the horizon, blending with distant mountains and the remainder of the day.

After finding Banyan's new headquarters, I stood at the Alden Memorial Hospital entrance glancing upward one more time before entering through the automatic sliding glass doors marked Emergency Entrance. I went in this way to observe the ER for future reference and to get a feel of where Banyan ended up after the chopper ride.

Several old people sat in the chairs that lined the stark white admitting area, a hall-like room that opened to an endless circular counter where a tall, slender nurse stood, asking if I needed help. I wanted to know where the ICU was. She pointed toward another hall with elevators, said it was on the third floor and went back to a harried but steady pace of studying charts and computer screens. There wasn't much to observe here. It was still early for the ER. Yet in another five hours daily routine would probably turn to pandemonium. The elderly people would be replaced with a younger crowd who would also be clinging to life.

It was dark and subdued in the ICU. There was a constant hum from the machinery behind another circular counter in the middle of the wing. I approached the nurses' station and asked a shorthaired, stocky Hispanic nurse, whose name tag said Anna, if I could see Banyan. She asked if I was family. I told her an extension of family. She told me no.

"I'm with the *Great Valley Beacon* and I thought Derrick might have something important to say," I patiently explained to the attending nurse. Then added pleadingly: "Derrick has a good rapport with the paper. I'm sure he'd like to see me if he's able." I was taking a huge leap with that line.

"You'll have to check with the supervisor when he returns from dinner," she said and excused herself by looking down at papers clipped to shiny sheet metal.

"What kind of shape is he in?" I said. "I had heard he has regained consciousness."

"He is improving. But again you'll have to speak to the one in charge for the specifics. We're really not allowed to comment, so please don't quote me in your article."

With time to kill, I called the office and told Jen the situation and that I'd be spending the night and not to expect me home for dinner. She may have said "fine" but she sounded ambivalent about the whole thing, especially expecting me home.

I headed downtown under the twilight sky to a well-known dive that served 'two-fers' and free appetizers till 7 P.M. Since I didn't have an expense account, when happy hour ran out, so did I, returning to the hospital and the male supervisor.

I knew from past experiences all gamblers are superstitious to a degree. They try to maintain control over their fate with esoteric techniques, like rituals performed by primitive tribes. They pluck the dice off the felt and throw in a style uniquely their own, as if methodology had control over the outcome. Some have lucky charms they carry around the neck or in pockets, or up sleeves. Nevertheless, cheating the system is hard, although it never deterred anyone from trying.

Banyan was cheating the system, the muscular nurse supervisor insinuated. He had once considered Banyan "a soul lost to this world." But the nurse exuberantly explained Banyan was regaining a form of consciousness; fingers touching the railing along his bed, rapid eye movement under his lids, and murmuring behind his lips.

"When do you think he'll be seeing visitors?" I asked.

"It's just immediate family for now," he said. "Maybe tomorrow if he is fully conscious. You're going to have to wait your turn though. Topping the list are the police who want to interview him first chance."

After leaving the hospital I headed toward the highway. Anywhere along the Interstate was a good place to shop for cheap motels. The Shady Spot had the lowest rate for a single business traveler like myself. After check-in I called Jen again to inform her of the status of things and then went to the bar across the street. It was a lifeless run-of-the-mill joint with low lights and dark burgundy decor. There were a few floozies at the bar with a guy who kept muttering, "I'm all fuckerdup" after every shot they downed. I guzzled the beer and realized it was time for some shuteye.

Sleep was as distant as the end of a boring movie I tried to watch. I finally shut off the tube and lay back in the dark hollow of a strange but familiar routine. I struggled with what direction to go in the Banyan story. The bed was uncomfortable and thoughts about writing news articles crisscrossed my mind like a New York City gridlock during rush hour. Maximum frustration was compounded by cognitive congestion until all of it coalesced into a dream.

Twisted bed sheets were wrapped around a hospital nightmare where colorless blood spewed out of patients dressed in white gowns. The spattered celluloid coated the dark floors of a hallway with nurses, imbedded like granite sentinels in the walls,

63

answering phones. The phones rang incessantly as Banyan kept wheeling himself down the hall toward me in a giant wheelchair-like bed. He never reached me because the ringing became louder, penetrating the dream world until it shattered the moment.

My first inclination was that it must be the wake-up call from the front desk. I reached for the noise, picked up the receiver and cradled it back to its base to silence the incessant ringing in my ears. The phone rang again a minute later. This time I held it to my head and listened for any sign of life on the other side.

"Spiver, you there?"

"I'm always here for you, baby."

"Why did you hang up on me a few moments ago. Am I disturbing anything important?" said Jen, in a chipper morning voice. I pictured her smiling, head tilting downward into the receiver, her hair cascading over her face making a veil of thin sandy brown strands.

"Sorry, I thought it was a wake-up call from the front desk."

"It is. What time would you prefer?"

"Uh, seven, maybe." I sounded sketchy even to myself.

"It's after eight. Rough night?"

"Not really, just bad dreams. But knowing you're on the line . . ."

"Rusty's here and wants to know what the plan is."

"I'll call in a report within the hour, whether Banyan is talking or not. I should be back before noon."

"I'll need a full story by eleven at the latest," said Jeannette in a straightforward voice that made me picture Rusty hovering close by. "We're planning to run everything you have on the front."

"Sure. But can we talk dirty real quick, before I have to take a cold shower?"

"Anything you say. So we'll expect you soon," said Miss Formality. "Got to run."

There are always subtle messages to be found on signs and ideograms along the road. When I saw the Kum & Go convenience store on my way to Alden Memorial it was clear I needed to stop and buy coffee, donuts, orange juice and gas. Then I saw a couple of newspaper boxes at every corner and finally bought a day-old *Crescent City News*.

When I got to the hospital there were several people I recognized in the waiting area of the ICU. The first one was Sally Sawmaker, working her magic for the *Crescent City News*. The others were familiar locals of Great Valley, friends and followers of Banyan's. Some acknowledged my presence by tilting their heads in my direction, others ignored me, including Sawmaker — until I took a seat next to her. I didn't deserve the silent treatment just because her paper had a larger circulation than the *Beacon*.

"Hello, Wily," she said, smiling, and turned her attention to a notebook she was studying.

"Hi, Sally. Enjoyed your story on the Sorrow Creek commissioner meeting. You really have a way of getting some good material out of those commissioners without attending any of those boring meetings."

"Thanks. I liked your stories also," she said, patronizing me. She put on such airs of superiority it obscured reality. Like pretending she wasn't lying to me.

I flipped through the paper Sally Sawmaker worked for, and read a day-old horoscope to see if there was any truth in it. Remarkably, it was close: *"You might have a difficult time buckling down. Popularity sours from lack of effort."* Only the stars knew what it would say about this particular day.

A water cooler gurgled in the corner as someone refilled a cup. There were about ten men and women spaced evenly apart in connected black chairs along the walls in the light beige waiting room. To pass the time, they read books or magazines, or glanced at a television morning show describing favorite summertime treats three weeks before summer arrived. I glanced at the clock.

It was a little past nine when I stood and started to wander around. I went past the elevators and walked down the hall to the end. A large window looked out across a landscape of a city with a palisade backdrop. The morning was shaping up to be a hot one as the few remaining clouds burned away below a glaring sun. Heat rippled off the surrounding buildings and the parking lot below where people — probably not wanting to be here either — moved listlessly around older cars and pickups. The town had been economically ravaged after the uranium, then oil shale and natural gas busts and it still showed the scars a half century later. If it had been a large Vegas hotel, the lot would have been littered with late model Cadillacs, Lexus' and other ostentatious rides in valet parking.

Instead, among the sea of aging hulks was a bright red Chevy Blazer with someone about to get in. The Blazer's roof prevented a view of everything but the fact that it was a slim woman who wore slacks and a dark gray sports jacket, an anomaly in a town where people mostly dressed in blue jeans.

I continued to scan the horizon with languid composure. Hospitals had that effect on me, unlike, let's just say, the frenzied state of a casino.

If someone bets against the players in a craps game, a negative energy field can come into play, scrambling the pattern of already uncertain consequences, like a radio operator jamming signals during an attack. Derrick Banyan was that guy who had stepped up to the table and laid down his chips against the status quo. Undoubtedly his opponents hoped he would cash out in dreamland.

And then thoughts on a rough draft for tomorrow's paper drifted aimlessly along bright green spherical treetops. Beyond the city limits was the dry reddish-brown desert with its barren cliffs and buttes. Even though it was late spring it felt like summer had come to Crescent City in full force. Before I went back to the waiting room, I scanned the parking lot again and noticed a Blazer-less space.

6

The coincidence of corresponding events could be an act in Greek mythology about the fates of man. The Greeks and Romans had three goddesses who controlled the lives of men: Clotho, who spun the web of life; Lachesis, who measured its length, and Atropos, who cut it.

When I found out Banyan had taken a U-turn on the road to recovery, it seemed like Atropos was Banyan's tailor that day. I stood among hordes of others surrounding the nurses' station, trying to make sense out of any thread of evidence being offered for the cause of Banyan's death.

A doctor emerged from Banyan's room and quickly began: "It appears that Derrick Banyan died from causes associated with the extensive injuries he sustained from the car accident. That's all we can say at this time. We'll keep you informed with any further details when we know them."

I scribbled the quote in my notebook and watched Sally Sawmaker press the doctor for more information. He held firm, fending off a barrage of questions, with: "We'll let you know when everything becomes apparent," and strode quickly toward Banyan's door with a couple of nurses in tow.

Momentarily my thought process hit a brick wall. I was dumfounded by the fact he had died in the short time I'd meditated before the window at the end of the hall.

I called Jen to let her know I'd file the story in short order.

"We all miss you, Wily, but I think Rusty misses your copy more. How soon can you get here?"

"As soon as my ass can sit down and file the story," I said. "Or I can dictate it to you."

"I know what your dick-tation means. So send it just as quick as you can. You got about a half hour."

"How long do you want it?" I said jokingly. Derrick Banyan's death looked routine enough, yet it would still make the full front page spread. "Want a couple of sidebars to go with it?"

"Make it as long as you can. But remember you only have thirty or forty minutes. You can give me the rest later." She hung up without saying goodbye, which didn't surprise me. She, too, was on deadline when tension began to mount like a volcano about to erupt.

The fact Derrick Banyan's death lingered on in the pages of *The Great Valley Beacon* for a week wasn't a surprise either. I had been scouring the archives for any story related to him. According to the old leather-bound copies of the *Beacon*, Banyan was a legend in environmental circles. In the short time since meeting him, I personally believed he was a saint of sorts in trying to save the planet by standing up to corporate polluters with their army of lawyers and lying propaganda experts.

First, I wrote a chronology of events leading to his demise, most of it derived from official statements from cops and doctors, sprinkled with community reactions. Then there was an expanded obituary.

Since he was considered a big-league activist and had picked Great Valley as his battleground, the feature obit ran as a center spread. Jim Tucker had recycled various pictures from the photo files, which revealed Banyan in action. One rectangular black and white showed him standing on the steps of the old brownstone courthouse giving two thumbs up to the small crowd surrounding him. The caption read: *Derrick Banyan emerged triumphant from the Great Valley Courthouse after a temporary injunction was issued to Skywest Ski Area. The court ordered a more comprehensive environmental impact study before logging operations could continue.*

The obligatory life history mostly highlighted his accomplishments as a conservation crusader. The coverage required little effort except connecting the dots – those short, concise sentences and paragraphs from past issues of *The Beacon*.

A sidebar covered a protest march he had led to halt a coal company from opening a mine in suburbia. The accompanying photo caught him in mid-stride, holding a placard stretched above his head: "Caution Wyocoal – Children at Play".

Since his latest assault on the corporate world was directed toward the Las Vegas developer, I mentioned it in a story about his memorial service:

Derrick vs. Goliath:
Banyan's Battle Lives On

Derrick Banyan was laid to rest yesterday at Long View Cemetery, but his vision for a better environment will live on, proclaimed a protégé of Banyan.

Over a hundred mourners stood in attendance at a memorial service held under a blistering sun at City Park. Acting Red River Coalition leader, Blanche Banyan, spoke of her husband's devotion to protecting the environment and seeking alternative energy sources to the prehistoric choices of today.

"It's time to move beyond fossil thinking which threatens the very conservation projects Derrick had vigorously worked to instill worldwide," said Blanche, standing at a walnut podium shaped like a coffin and ringed with wildflowers, pine saplings and other potted plant life.

"In the spirit of Derrick's goals and ambitions, we will continue his fight to protect the future from catastrophe. The Red River Coalition, with well over a thousand members nationwide, stands as testament to his legacy," added Ms. Banyan before a crowd that applauded energetically.

Derrick Banyan's most recent battle against his alleged corporate wrongdoers ended in a fight with an official spokesman for a Las Vegas development company after a recent county commissioner meeting.

According to a Great Valley police report, Derrick Banyan was involved in an altercation with Victor Saville, representative for Nevada Resorts International (NRI). Saville and Banyan came to blows after a commissioner meeting two days prior to his death.

The Las Vegas company is actively working on a lease agreement with Omni Oil Corporation for its land and water rights to develop the Sorrow Creek Basin. Plans include an 800-acre reservoir along with a 1,600-unit housing project called Glenn Eden Resort.

The leisure community will also feature an 18-hole championship golf course, tennis courts and an Olympic-sized swimming pool with clubhouse.

Derrick Banyan was opposed to damming Sorrow Creek at the meeting. He also protested the concept of leasing water rights to an out-of-state entity. The reservoir will be used as water storage for NRI's water allocation in Nevada, primarily for a hotel and casino resort.

"What's this about Victor Saville again?" asked Jen, after proofreading the copy.

"What about him?" I got up from my desk and walked all of fifty steps over to read what she was talking about.

She said, "The implication that Saville might have something to do with Banyan's death. Isn't that pushing the limit in an obit?"

"So that's what you think I'm implying?"

"In ways I am sure you're totally aware of," she said. "There'll be a lot of people at issue with it if Rusty lets it run. And not only Saville, but I'm pretty sure Blanche as well."

I had bent over her right shoulder to see the copy on the computer screen. The fragrance of her shampoo smelled like a bouquet of jasmine as I focused on her blossoming cleavage, slightly exposed by an undone button of her yellow blouse.

"The only thing I am aware of is you."

"Stop that or you'll get us both in trouble."

She was more than tempted to cut the part about Saville out so I said, "I know it's kind of a stretch, but what the hell, there *might* be a connection."

"I guess you might say it's a news-obit of the likes I've never seen before. In my opinion Saville ought to roast in Las Vegas. What do they think, that Sorrow Creek is their watering trough?" She answered her own question. "Hell no. What he's proposing is crazy, and if Banyan died in some way because of it, then we have a duty to print it." She said it straight-faced, making it hard to tell if she was serious or not. "But who's to say there's not a hit man for the oil company after Banyan? I can't believe you haven't stuck that in the mix since you seem to be turning into a tabloid journalist on us."

Old habits are hard to break, I thought. During my copywriting experience in Vegas I was taught by my mentor and publisher of *Vegas Vanity*, Rudy Morris, that I was in the business to tantalize readers.

Maybe my story was inappropriate for an obituary or I was leading readers along with a biased viewpoint. Another thing I didn't tell Jeannette was I had known Vegas types my whole life and most of them could have been exposed in an investigation. But I'd let Rusty and Jen decide what needs exposing. So all I said in response was, "Whatever the cause, I'm sure Banyan didn't die in vain."

"And whatever that is it will have to wait for another day." She smiled then, looked around the empty office. "How come we're always the last to leave? Let's put a wrap on it. I'm hungry."

To chill out from the intense June heat that had permeated the office, Jeannette suggested dinner at Pitt's BBQ Barn. The spot with the least grease stains.

Jen and I walked in the twilight's soft orange hue along Progress Avenue to the bar and restaurant. Inside Pitt's, the AC wasn't producing the desired effect. We tried to order quickly from a waitress who had a frazzled way of avoiding us, and sat listening to the noisy hum of a faulty air conditioner until I broke the monotony with: "Where'd the waitress go?"

"Who cares? I don't think we are making her day. I'm not all that hungry now anyway."

"I thought you were the one who wanted to come here. What's up?"

"I lost my appetite thinking about domestic tranquility." She did a mock frown and added, "Isn't that an oxymoron if it's without sex?"

I was momentarily speechless. She had aroused my interest, and as a result I had a blatant disregard for the sweltering atmosphere. An electrical charge flashed on the horizon of my thoughts as if there was an approaching storm.

She faked a frown and pouted, "It's not fair." And looked as if she was also beginning to feel the chemical change in the air.

"To who? Or you mean the lack of sex?" I was stimulated by Jen's gale force stare. How else to describe it but in terms of a fast approaching storm without warning. Her eyes were like hurricanes, a blue calm with cloudless centers, and all the energy to cause tidal waves of desire.

"To everyone involved," she said.

"Then let's make love to even things out." I would've liked more verbal foreplay instead of what I thought was a bittersweet come-on.

"Is that your answer?" Jen asked without hesitation.

I tried plying her with humor. "Or treat yourself to a divorce. It's all the rage."

"That's not the problem. Anyway, I don't want to talk about it now."

She fidgeted with the silverware while I got someone to serve us.

We ate in silence, digesting our affinity for each other as well as our differences.

"Linda considers you a drifter," Jen finally said. Linda Duncan was the *Beacon*'s ad manager and hadn't taken to me at all. "Linda says women shouldn't get involved with guys like you. Says you aren't the kind to stick around for very long. Is that true?"

"I didn't know she knew me that well. We're only around each other in passing. I've hardly ever spoken to her. But you two are friends, right?"

Jen didn't answer the question. "She's right though."

"If that's what she thinks, I'd say she was looking out for your interests," I blurted out in frustration.

"Yeah, well, I need to deal with this divorce thing anyhow," she said with a nonchalance that scorched the playing field.

"Then why the hell are you concerned whether or not I stay?"

"So you would leave me behind?" She laughed. "I'm just toying with you, Wily. Quit being so serious."

At that moment we were both sharing the same unsettling universe in Great Valley. Since even our conversation lacked any sense of stability, I suggested she come to my place. She frowned.

"Is that all you care about, having sex?"

"What's wrong with that?" I asked, wondering if somehow I'd misread the situation.

"You're right. We're becoming too involved," she said.

"You see, it's not just sexual since we haven't done anything."

"So what's wrong with that," she said with mock amusement.

"It's hot in here," I said irritably. "Dinner was probably a mistake. I'd better be off." Melodramatic moments had never been my specialty, so I said anything to get past the awkwardness. Even though we were friends, it felt like my other past relationships. They had eventually fallen apart when the glue that bonds them became cracked or brittle.

But she reached across the table, tightening her hand around my forearm. "Okay. It's getting too heated in here anyway. Let's meet at your place in about fifteen minutes."

"Anything you want. What about your husband?"

"He's probably screwing the secretary. He took her with him."

I paid the check and drove to my room. It was a relief to see the owner of the Lucky U, Eloy Munn, managing the front desk instead of Lucy as I drove eyeballing past the lobby and around back.

When Jen showed up, I pulled two beers from the mini-fridge while she reclined slightly on the bed. Her lips were wet from the froth off the top of the longneck bottle as we engaged in enthusiastic kissing; then we laid side by side against each other on the queen spread and began tugging on any loose clothing until nothing was left to hold but flesh. It became one of those sublime moments. The stimulating eroticism Jen generated was a diversion from what otherwise could have been a deepening abyss with a married woman.

Making it vexing though, were small facts and revelations — like Jeannette's desire to cheat on her husband. And that I was just an easy lay, filling in the gap for her sexual frustration. But then, did I really care? I had always liked chance possibilities from a distance, treading cautiously when involved with the opposite sex.

Afterward, we kissed briefly in the motel parking lot while our eyes darted around, looking to see who in the Lucky U neighborhood might have observed us.

7

I was finishing the night with a tall scotch on the rocks and HBO in the dark hollows of my motel room, a place only mushrooms could appreciate, when a knock landed on the door. I wondered why cheap motels have peepholes, but went to see who was standing in the hall anyway.

If I had a choice, I probably wouldn't have a peephole. I'd seen enough of the occupants of the Lucky U just walking the halls that I didn't need a window out into that world. But reality stepped in when the knocking persisted. There was Victor Saville staring into the peephole. Christ, I couldn't believe it. Should I stand at the door in silence and act as if I didn't see anything. Or yell something like, "Who is it?"

"Open up, Spiver, I know you're in there. It's Saville."

Sure enough, when I opened the door, there stood Wicked Vic, big as life, like a menacing cloud obscuring the hallway. He was dressed like he always was, in the dark blue pinstripe suit, always playing the type, even if he was in a town that probably didn't sell ties, let alone suits.

The sight was an extreme contrast to the hour before when Jen had left. Instead of reveling about naked, I stood repulsed at what the storm unleashed. "What brings you to this particular door, Vic?"

He said, "In the neighborhood and thought I'd stop by for a little chat."

"I would've thought you had your fill of the riffraff around here after the fight with Banyan," I said while standing in the door, puzzled whether to invite him in.

"Never give up on that, do you, Spiver?" he said. "And by the way, it was a tragic loss. We may have had our differences, but there was a certain respect I had for the guy. Now do the same and let it rest." He had the look of a humorless human being, but feigned a smile anyway. "Give it some serious thought. You might say that your future here is on the line."

"What's that supposed to mean?"

"You know what I mean. I have a low tolerance for this kind of shit you're pulling. "

Vic didn't give a rat's ass about Derrick Banyan. He may not have killed Banyan, but then again, I wouldn't have put it past him to have made the necessary arrangements. The way with a Vegas type like him was usually to eliminate the problem instead of tolerating it.

Only this was the New West, where one tended not to believe in the ways of old. Derrick Banyan hadn't cared if he was up against Genghis Khan. From what I'd learned since being in Great Valley, he had been brazen enough to take on a variety of land and water developers in spite of local support against his crusade, a regular Napoleon Banyan with an empire founded on environmental issues.

"So what's up, Vic, with the Sorrow Creek deal?" I asked, hoping to change the subject. "I'd really like to get an exclusive interview with you to balance out the coverage, instead of you avoiding me."

"This is it: Everything you need to know is in the press releases. No way you're getting any special privileges. And I really don't give a shit who your dad is."

"So you know him too."

"*So you know him too!* You son of a bitch; why'd you lie about it when I asked if you two were related?" He said it with a vicious growl as if emulating a wild beast about to attack.

I recognized intimidation when I saw it and really didn't need any dramatics, but I took the threat seriously and tried persuading him to back off. "There's nothing to worry about there, we like keeping clear of each other's business."

"Good. I don't think he'd care too much for bad news."

I couldn't be sure how my father would react if he thought his son was acting incongruously. It had been over a year since we had last seen each other, when we met at one of the casinos he managed. He looked unaffected by the business, in fact, looked even better through the years. When I told him that, he said: "The secret to my longevity has always been to challenge the odds by knowing how to play what's dealt to you. It helps relieve the pressure by being prepared. Who needs a lot of unwanted stress?" He took a sip of champagne, then continued in this kind of gambling philosophy he enjoyed expounding on. "In poker or craps, it's being aware of the action with a callous eye. In life, it's fighting the demons at the door instead of letting them in." He actually said this a year earlier, as if he were a clairvoyant. Or in my case, telepathic because here stood a demonic character if ever I saw one.

For a public relations person, Vic wasn't too personable or public. He stood at the door with all the intention of intimidation and was doing a damn good job of it. "Look, Vic, I'd rather deal with any problem you have with me on a personal level. One on one," I said.

"Stick to the Sorrow Creek deal and we're all set." He grinned with the secure feeling look that everything was under his control. Of course this didn't come as a surprise to me since my mentor, the great adult entertainment publisher, Rudy Morris, had always told me the gambling industry didn't like publicity unless it was in the form of positive advertising.

Even if he didn't know anything about PR, Victor Saville understood the importance of diplomacy as a way of masking his true intentions. "Just so you got it clear in that thick skull of yours, I don't appreciate you mentioning the scuffle between Banyan and myself in the paper. No one should get the wrong impression. Understand?" Vic was still standing in the doorway, his girth almost filled it completely. Since he didn't smile, I regarded this advice as deadly serious.

"Look Vic," I said, "By all accounts, Banyan's death was an accident. There wasn't anything in the article accusing anyone of murder."

"Except by implication."

"If that's what you read, then I apologize for any misunderstanding."

I looked into his dark beady eyes for a reaction, but only saw a sliver of white, refracted, fluorescent light from the hallway. He didn't squint or blink, but stared back with indifference. "We have somewhat of a working relationship here; don't let it rot any further. That way nobody has to worry about spoilage," he said with a stoicism that made his statuesque build look like it was made of granite. Whether or not the rough contoured rock would shatter if he ever moved again, I wasn't sure. He then cracked a calculating grin. "Good job on getting the word out about the Sorrow Creek resort."

I said, "Thanks to your press releases. The commissioners are all over the proposal."

His grin reduced to a perplexing horizon, dividing a sadistic smile and deep anger. At eye level, we were the same height, but not the same size. He must have had a good eighty pounds on me, plus a few pounds more with all the clothes he was wearing and the concealed weapon. I was defenseless in a tee shirt, jeans and socks over my hundred-seventy-pound frame. "Sorry I didn't dress for the occasion, but do you want a drink or something?"

"This isn't a social call. I just wanted to get clear on the situation before it got too late. Sleep well," he said and strode off across the hall toward his room. I glanced at my digital watch, it read 12:10. It was later than I thought, but getting some shuteye didn't cross my mind.

* * *

My biggest mystery wasn't Victor Saville, but Derrick Banyan. Was he so important someone had to kill him? He never posed any real threat to the Sorrow Creek Project. At least that was the way it appeared on the surface.

But in the case of Victor Saville, my jury had him pegged. It only took me two minutes of deliberation and a scotch on the rocks to figure the guy guilty of some duplicitous deed involving the Sorrow Creek development. It may have only been circumstantial evidence, but made even more evident by Saville's appearance before my court of personal involvement. I poured out another shot to steady my nerves and thought, nobody tampers with the media *except* maybe the Mafia and corrupt corporations.

The media is supposed to be immune to gossip, subjective reporting and veiled threats. At least that's what every delusional reporter wanted to believe. My apparition had knocked on a door with a creep hole to view the specter. It wasn't until I was face to face with reality that I was able to meditate on the meaning of it all. How had I arrived in a situation where my life became entangled in the web of a poisonous spider?

In a way I just wanted to cut free of the mess by leaving Great Valley. I collapsed across the bed and stared up at the ceiling. Thoughts about Victor Saville's visit were cobwebs in the corners of my mind like the ones in my room. And I really didn't want to be caught in his web.

As a means of escape, I found myself reliving my early years in Vegas when I was a blackjack dealer. I worked at the old Cabana Hotel, in its garish Havana-style casino. Its Cuban theme was almost convincing enough to believe you were in another country, where management was mostly of Spanish or Puerto Rican decent. It was pleasant enough. Card tables and slot machines blended nicely with the floral patterned carpet of broad red leaves and green ferns. Ornamental palms were lined against the stucco walls with a facade of a Spanish barrio to make you think it was Cuba in the nineteen-fifties. The rumba dancers performed on stage in the lounge and later in my sleep.

The following morning Jeannette called and wanted to know why I was late. "I understand you cover meetings lasting all night. But there wasn't any last night, Spiver," she said in a demanding voice. "It looks bad to certain staff members, you always wandering in later than the rest of us."

At that moment I made the mistake of letting out a yawn. So she fired back with, "What, am I boring you? Rusty's here and was wondering about the obit you wrote." No wonder she was being such a hard ass. Rusty was pressing on her.

"You're never boring. It's that I didn't get much rest after Victor Saville came by around 'bout midnight. Wouldn't that qualify as a late night meeting?"

"What did *he* want?" She started to lighten up.

"I suppose you could call it doing a welfare check." I was starting to sound like a cop report. A welfare check was what cops did when checking on someone that somebody said needed looking in on. It's not necessarily a big city cop function. When I first heard the term, I assumed someone was missing his or her welfare check.

"Did you need looking after last night?" she said half-jokingly, half-serious.

"Give me a break; I was a good boy until I met Darth Vader. The evil empire has found me."

"If you mean by this phone call . . ."

"No, no, I mean —" And what did I mean, I wasn't sure myself.

"All right, Wily, we all miss you at work," she said sarcastically. "Is that better? Now get your butt down here so you can find out what a bad boy you are."

I hung up, then took a long hot shower, followed by a quick cold one, trying to cleanse away all traces of last night. I may have been cleaner, but there was a residue to the morning thought process the sandman wouldn't relinquish. With a white towel wrapped around my waist, I stood in front of the dresser mirror and studied the savage and ravaged reflection before carefully picking out my wardrobe, which was crammed in the three drawers below.

The day had the potential for being filled with promise. Too bad I didn't feel the energy to pursue it. It was nine o'clock, with a chance of rain in the forecast, blared the radio announcer of KUNTRY 55 AM. It was the only available station on the battered clock radio that still played songs instead of syndicated talk and religious programming. Yippie-ki-ay! I was in cowboy heaven.

After quickly dressing, I slid open the drapes and inspected the glass. It was still intact, which was more than I could say about my brain. I scanned the landscape and parking lot below, which produced a sort of déjà vu, besides a headache.

The morning's gray glare made it difficult to see anything but random patterns; dark clouds against a silvery sky, parked cars against black asphalt, outlines of green trees against green fields and roads between the glints of intermittent traffic. I stared a while longer in search of the vague familiarity until spotting the source, a red Chevy Blazer, similar to the one seen at the hospital.

I grabbed my binoculars off the dresser and aimed them at the parking lot. The lineup of letters, ZLR, meant rental tags from the only agency in town.

By the time I ambled out of my room and into the parking lot, the Blazer had vanished. I approached the motel lobby hoping to see Lucy's bright, smiling face behind the counter, but instead there was the sneering countenance of the owner, Eloy Munn. The unexpected sight sent me reeling back into the parking lot to my car. I had hoped Lucy could tell me who owned the Blazer; fat chance that Eloy Munn would.

So I drove to a bygone Phillips 66 gas station, which housed the car rental agency. The building's architecture was '60s style, when stations had that cantilevered look to them. The triangular metal canopy, which once spanned gas pumps, was now used to house a variety of late model cars including some SUVs.

Inside belied any sign of a former gas station. It was carpeted in red. The office area extended out to where the mechanic bays once were, with several partitions separating desks.

A woman in her early thirties greeted me with a friendly smile. "I was curious about renting one of those Blazers," I said in an attempt to ease into what I really came for.

"By the day or week? And we have long term programs available if you're interested in leasing." She quickly exchanged her cheerful smile with a quizzical one. "You work for the paper, don't you?"

"Maybe. It all depends on whether I have a job or not when I get back." I didn't know most of the locals I ran into, unless I could attach them to what they did for a living.

"Jen is my cousin. I'm Lisa, and you must be Wily. Jen told me about you."

"Nice to meet you." I said. "I was wondering if you rent red Chevy Blazers."

"We've only got one in stock and it's been rented."

"When will it become available?" I asked.

"I can't really say, I think it's an open-ended contract. There are other vehicles available."

"But no red Blazers? I really had my mind set on the one I see around town. If I had his name maybe he could be talked into an exchange. I think we're staying at the same place."

"Then ask that person. But we don't divulge any customer information, unless you are the police." She made it seem like a firm denial.

"It's part of a story I'm working on. I'm sure Jen would appreciate the favor, just this once."

"In that case, I can't see the harm of telling you she's from Washington, D.C. But that's all I can say without getting into some serious trouble. Tell Jen I said hi and I'll see her later." And we left it at that.

The sun was partially eclipsed by a dark cloud when I parked across the street from the office and then waited to cross Progress Avenue. Even after I took off my shades, everything swam in the hazy soup of ambiguity. I promised myself to keep the hangover to a minimum in the future. At the moment I had to deal with a fast approaching deadline as well as a fuzzy outlook.

Something was amiss when I saw Jeannette standing outside waiting for a parade of cars to pass. She wasn't the kind to idle during work. She smiled when she saw me, but under that pleasant greeting there was a look of concern or annoyance.

"Wait there," she yelled.

I watched the familiar cars and trucks roll by, often with an uncanny resemblance to their occupants — a similar link dog owners have with their pets. Progress Avenue sometimes offered a dim view of the day's activities. Observing downtown life either improved or impeded progress depending on the story angle, and what was being covered and who the main characters were.

When she finally got a break in the traffic, Jen crossed over, and said in a clear voice, "Wily, it's late. I thought you were coming in immediately. Are you okay?"

"I got a little diverted. Can we talk about it inside? I've got a feeling I need to sit for this one."

"Rusty's pissed you weren't here for the editorial meeting. If you go in there now looking like death warmed over, he'll come uncorked. He was thinking of firing you after he met with that character Victor Saville. But I insisted you were more of an asset than a liability," She smiled, then added "Which I know is an understatement. Anyhow, I told him you were at an interview for Friday's feature and he left with Saville."

"Fair enough." Although I felt deflated, it was just a minor inconvenience in the scheme of things. Victor Saville paid Rusty a visit and possibly more. Although she didn't know where they went, apparently the editorial meeting between Jen, Saville and Gates set off a chain reaction of events that ultimately led to Rusty's rant about firing me.

Jen had overruled Gates with the argument I had been working hard on the angle that Banyan's demise was probably foul play. It got Rusty's attention and that was all it took to calm him down.

"Jesus, Jen. I got nothing close to concrete, let alone a solid angle yet."

"I know. But who else besides me is going to watch out for your sweet little ass? Meanwhile, get out there and come up with something tangible. And I need one of those back burner features you've been stockpiling. See you later this afternoon."

"I'll put something together, but it might not be what you had in mind."

"What's that mean?"

"I ran into your cousin, Lisa, at her office. She told me to say hi to you."

Jeannette walked back into the office. I crossed the street to the doughnut hut for some brown doughnuts, black coffee and lots of white sugar. I waited for the energy boost to kick in, but all I felt was the presence of Joe as he moved slowly behind the counter refilling coffee cups with inky fluid.

Lucy walked in and sat next to me at the counter. Joe leaned forward across the counter and greeted her with a hug; in turn she kissed him on the cheek. They were old friends in a small town. To be considered a local in Great Valley, you had to be pretty tied into the community in some way, related or not. Joe probably had known Lucy since she had been a kid, and watched her grow into a robust woman who loved singing. If he knew Lucy that well, he'd know she had talent going to waste while working long hours at the registration desk.

"Howdy stranger," said Lucy with a direct focus at my appearance. "You look like shit."

"Hi, Lucy. What's up?" I stared back, looking for clues on how to respond to her delicate description of my condition.

"You know, the usual. Waiting by the front door for you to come home. Not." She laughed. "I wouldn't be there if it wasn't required. And how are you?"

"Busy. News never lets up as long as Great Valley is in motion."

We sat at the counter, side by side, and watched Joe's thick hairy arm reach out and pour Lucy some coffee. "Is that why I haven't seen you around much?" she asked.

"Yeah, that and all the late night meetings and early deadlines. Where does the time go?"

"I'd say screwing Jeannette LaBreeze." She directed her words toward the kitchen area where Joe's fry order cook stood before the grill turning out eggs and pancakes, and then setting everything under a heat lamp, oblivious to the dining room chatter.

"Whoa, where did you get an impression like that?"

"My imagination. Where do you think, Wily? Eloy says he saw her going into your room."

"Pretty vivid imagination." I watched Lucy's long fingers, made even longer by her well-manicured fingernails, grasp the white porcelain coffee mug for a sip.

"I figure it's part of your nature, so I won't hold it against you."

"What's that supposed to mean?"

"I know we're just friends, but I thought I meant more to you than an interim lay until you found someone else."

"If you're pissed about us, I'm sorry. I always thought of it as a mutual-benefit fling without attachments."

"Are you calling me a slut?"

"Never."

"Then I'll forgive you if you tell me what's wrong with attachment." She was staring earnestly with those beautiful dark eyes into mine.

"It's just I'm kind of afraid of commitment. And Jeannette . . ."

"Jesus, Wily, she's still married. Besides, she's not your type. Trust me on that one."

I couldn't decide if it was the cloudy weather or my thinking process that diminished the morning brightness as minutes ticked away at Joe's.

91

Lucy moved through the motions, pushing for details when there was only obscurity. Guilt surfaced in my subconscious like the rising smoke off a nearby cigarette smoldering unattended in a glass ashtray.

"What are you doing tonight?" she said between sips of coffee.

"Probably working, like most other nights."

"Me too. Why don't you come by the desk afterward?"

"I'm kind of occupied," I tried to be smooth about it, not wanting to lose her as a friend.

"We're all preoccupied with something, Wily. Besides, I'm the one who pulls that chain," she said, possibly alluding to the neon glow in the window of a motel lobby turning people away.

Lucy was wearing a necklace against a black V-neck shirt tucked into well fitting blue jeans. I couldn't keep my eyes off the turquoise stones, framed in silver, resting against her breasts. It was an Indian piece with a bear fetish that could have been for luck. "Come by the front desk when you're done with work or whatever. I like seeing you when we can spend time together."

This kind of talk always got a rise out of me. Then Lucy pushed her leg up against mine as if in need of support, her thigh sliding along mine when she stood to leave. I just sat and wondered. Then she winked and grinned at me.

"Before you leave could you tell me who drives that red Blazer I saw in the parking lot this morning?"

She scanned the cafe to avoid looking down at me. "Some chick. Why, you got the hots for her too?"

"No, not that. I'm just curious, that's all. Do you remember her name?"

"P.I. Privileged Information. See you tonight and we can share secrets." She left it at that and headed toward the door, through the morning flurry of chattering voices and clattering plates, without looking back.

8

I pushed the doughnut shop sounds off to the edge of my brain and filled the void with thoughts like what a great woman Lucy was to me, what directed fate, and what were the odds of chance encounters against orchestrated ones.

Some people, like Charlie Ray, had a grasp on it. Ray was an apprentice scientific-instrument maker who was encouraged by San Francisco gamblers to create the mechanical three-reeler, known later as the slot machine.

Charlie Ray was the inventor of this well-orchestrated payoff, a machine programmed to substantially favor the house. An endless stream of money poured into these machines from people who should have known better than to hold out hope that their next spin would wheel them to fortune. This also could be compared to the sucker bet, though eventually, somebody beats the odds in a chance encounter with the slots.

As much as I tried avoiding any encounters with Lucy since becoming involved with Jen, inevitable opportunities were overwhelmingly present, whether orchestrated or not.

After leaving Joe's, I walked back along Progress Avenue thinking of some feature I was supposed to have in the wings. It had been sprinkling, and the smell of wetness and car fumes permeated the air until the clouds began to burn off. Soon the temperature would be a baking 95 degrees. Not a big deal for someone who grew up in Vegas. However, there were substantial differences. In Vegas, you had the air-conditioned life, an escape from the sweltering realities of Litter Gulch and Lost Wages. In Great Valley, the defenses weren't as fortified and meltdowns were more common.

To avoid any kind of meltdown at the office I decided to work from home, and maybe corner Lucy on the driver of the Blazer.

Eloy Munn was on duty at the counter. He glared at *Days in Our Lives* and looked mesmerized by what sounded like a woman's tumultuous affair unraveling with all the venomous anger of a rattlesnake being shoved into a burlap bag by a malicious poacher.

"Hey Eloy," I interrupted, "Is Lucy around?"

"Down the hall."

I walked down the wing Eloy pointed to and found Lucy standing in a doorway, about to put the finishing touches on a room she had been cleaning.

"You're early," she said, rummaging through the maid cart, grabbing soap and towels. "I didn't expect you until *after* work."

"I couldn't wait. I really need to know who drives the Blazer."

"Sorry. No can tell. Come by tonight when I have access to the registration cards."

"It's for a story I'm working on right now."

Lucy smiled and pulled me part way into the cool, vacant room by reaching around my neck and drawing me in for a kiss. Then gave me a big hug. "I am working right now too," she said, "but it doesn't mean we can't have fun doing it."

"All right, I'll be by tonight," I said, trying to free myself from her grasp until she dropped her arms and pushed me back. Someone was walking down the hall toward us. The sound of steps echoed off the walls. It could have been a pissed off Munn.

Whoever it was, Lucy took it seriously enough to quickly compose herself and move toward the door, partially blocked by the large steel maid cart. Before she reached the hall, the phone rang beside the bed that remained neatly made. She changed direction and walked to the phone, sitting on the edge of the bed and picking up the receiver. Munn told Lucy someone from the paper just called my room.

The approaching mystery guest had abruptly stopped, and a door opened and closed.

"It was your editor who phoned," fumed an angry Munn as I passed through the lobby toward the stairs. He wasn't happy about taking the message. "Don't expect me to tell you every time someone calls. An answering service is not an option here."

That was a lie. Munn answered, routed, and most likely, monitored every call that came in and out of the motel.

I jogged to my room and called Jen back. She wasn't in a good mood either, but with her it was more in a detached way than confrontational.

"What's up?" I said between the pants in my heavy breathing.

She responded nonchalantly. "We're having another editorial meeting, which involves you, in a half hour. So get your cute little butt back down here." She paused, then added, "you sound out of breath. What were you up to when I called? Your landlord sounded really pissed."

"He hates being disturbed during *Days In Our Lives.*" I said to quickly end the conversation and avoid stray intonations. "I'll be there in about fifteen."

I rushed to shave and changed into a clean shirt and khakis, and then went to the window and scanned the parking lot below. There were about seven vehicles in the lot including my Trans Am and the red Blazer. When reaching the asphalt, I casually walked by the SUV, glancing in the windows for clues. The gray interior was clutter-free except for a brown leather briefcase on the passenger seat and a dark blue duffel-like nylon bag behind the back seat.

The morning fog had lifted from my brain and I started feeling better. I had a sense everything was under control, at least my version of control. The Blazer was a clue that things were shaping up after I decided there might be a connection to the vehicle and Banyan's fate. I knew it was a long shot at best.

The staff had congregated in the large production area. The three ad sales women, Linda

97

Duncan, Mary Middleton and LeAnn Shoe, and two other women, Tracy Martin and Diane Lopez, from production, sat on one side of the room. The editorial staff of Jim Tucker, Jen and I sat on the other. Rusty stood in the middle. The pressman and his assistant were excluded because of mechanical problems with the aging presses.

I tried sitting quietly during the staff meeting as Rusty explained any rumor about the paper being sold was false. Whoa, that's a shock, I thought. And judging by everyone's expression, it surprised them as well. "Of course, everything has its price and if someone were to offer a substantial amount, I'd consider selling," he added.

"What are you saying, Rusty? That we're maybe out of a job?" asked Tucker.

"No one's tendered an offer, yet."

The way I figured it, Rusty Gates already had a buyer lined up and the meeting was a smoke screen. He confirmed my sentiment by declaring a new and improved newspaper was now the main goal, starting with the banner and page layouts. Nothing more than window dressing, really. He wasn't going to increase the staff size, just the work load.

He explained that it was production's job to come up with the new format. The editorial department needed to encapsulate nonessential news stories and break major stories down into sidebars and shadow boxes with easily explainable facts, figures and graphics. Essentially this was news made into easy-to-digest pabulum, in a manner being emulated by papers all over the country. "Fancy graphics that will make it shine," he said.

Rusty immediately wanted to know what stories were on tap. He looked at me, applying pressure to break an awkward silence. Jen chimed in with a list, which included the gambling initiative and any Sorrow Creek updates.

The special election for the proposed gambling initiative was approaching and things had started to heat up between land speculators and angry opponents against a Sin City. Tucker had been handling the beat, but some of the work was to be shifted in my direction.

"Wily, how's the investigation into Banyan's death going?" He drifted over to one of the old production layout tables to sit on a high stool and smoke a cigarette. Everyone turned in my direction, expecting a revelation.

"The case is still open and the cops aren't making much headway. I'll follow-up with what I got so far."

"Exciting stuff." Rusty let out a yawn and mashed his cigarette out. It was illegal to smoke in a public place or office, but he didn't care. He said it was his business, not the government's. And if an employee complained, they could find a job elsewhere.

"I'll make it as lively as possible," I said, trying to sound interested in all the enthusiasm Rusty had for the paper's future, but failing.

He squinted in the lingering smoke and said, "If it's not too much to ask."

Apparently it was a running joke. Everyone in the room chuckled, even Jen. Gates was obviously pleased with that bit of humor. For me, it came as a warning that everyone was as bored with the lack of riveting news as I was. We had run with every possible angle in Banyan's case except closure. I looked in Jeannette's direction for moral support.

"Don't take it wrong, Wily," she injected softly. "We think you have your good moments; we just want to see more of them. Like more in depth gambling stories and some more about Saville's long range plans. Rusty seems to think we've only barely scratched the surface."

Rusty confirmed it with, "Let's put a wrap on Banyan's coalition and report on what's really starting to happen around here."

The meeting finally lurched forward like a stuck vehicle eventually freeing itself from a quagmire. Meetings were always like that though, especially if you were subjected to any kind of employee scrutiny. Gates concluded by saying the paper was going to run an election special.

Moans were heard throughout the room, except from the advertising side, the only group whose paycheck would increase from the extra commissions of selling ads around the special section. For everyone else, it was double the workload without any compensation except the gratification one gets from such worthy endeavors.

"And we are going to have a circulation contest with free vacation give-aways to the first ten subscribers that draw the winning tickets. It's an all-expense paid trip to Laughlin, Nevada," he told the group.

Jen piped in with, "you mean first ten *people*."

"Yeah, that's what I said," said Rusty.

"You said subscribers. The contest has to be open to anyone twenty-one years of age. Read the fine print."

"I read it, okay. But it's really more about the first ten who come up with the five hundred dollar buy-in. That's also in the fine print, along with a refund if they want to give back the casino chips when they leave. Totally legal says my lawyer."

After the meeting we drifted back to our individual work areas. I caught up with Jen at her desk. She was reading something off the computer screen. I asked her what she meant by my good moments. She looked up and laughed, telling me not to take it too seriously and that I should already know what she meant.

Coyly staring at me, she said in almost a whisper, "actually, it wasn't your writing I was referring to. Besides I was just trying to get Rusty off your ass."

"Thanks. I have to admit, it *was* becoming a little uncomfortable."

"You ain't seen nothin' yet, darling. Got a moment?" She turned toward her computer and printed out a staff memo outlining assignments and deadlines for the editorial department. "Rusty wants a head start on these stories for the election section."

"I can't wait to get started. What are you doing tonight?"

"Working," she said and returned her gaze to the computer screen.

"Why don't we have dinner later?"

"Can't," she said flatly.

"You have to eat sometime."

"Wily, let's hold off going out until after this election issue is in the can."

"Sure, but you'll get hungry before then." I smiled, and then let the dinner invitation drop.

What I didn't want to let go was Jen's comment about my news coverage. "You said I'm barely scratching the surface. What was that supposed to mean, by the way, or was that Rusty's observation?"

"I don't know. Sometimes I think Rusty's more interested in collecting insider info than uncovering any illegal activity perpetrated in the newspaper's community. You know Rusty, what he does with this knowledge depends largely on how it affects his personal finances."

"Obviously you know him a lot better than I do. But it doesn't surprise me. I know a publisher in Las Vegas, the one I worked for, felt the same way— that's because he published adult entertainment magazines."

"Look Wily, you should go talk to Rusty if it's bothering you. I've got work to do."

I watched Gates with vague apprehension as he blew smoke in my direction and became preoccupied with the mail pile atop his desk. He spread the envelopes around until he pulled out and unfolded a brown antique-looking flyer.

"Here, take a look at this. I want to make it into a full page ad promoting the contest." It was a map of Nevada with a large star indicating Laughlin's location. A heavy black banner headline in an Old-West font said it was a treasure map to the hidden riches of Nevada.

"Like I told you, we're going to start a circulation contest with the winners getting a weekend stay in Laughlin," Gates said. "I have business acquaintances that fly charter planes out of the Greater Valley Regional Airport to some of the smaller gambling towns, like Laughlin and Reno. The flyer is a promotional from my Laughlin buddies. They're the ones sponsoring the round-trip airfare and two nights lodging at the Moulin for the winners. All I've got to do is provide the advertising for it."

Jim Tucker had told me about the connection between the newspaper and the charter service a couple of days prior. He said that it wasn't hard to piece together, since Gates' main preoccupation, besides women, was gambling.

We were still discussing the trip give-away when Jeannette paged Rusty on the intercom, saying a woman from the charter service was on line two. From bits and pieces of conversation, I understood Gates was to leave Friday afternoon, standby; meaning free if there was a seat available. I got up to leave, but he signaled for me to sit and indicated he'd be off the phone soon. He jabbered on a few more minutes about scheduling and times, then said, "See you this weekend" into the receiver before hanging up.

"Uuuuh, where was I?" he asked. Then, answering his own question: "Oh, yeah, the promotion. That can wait. We need to keep on top of the Sorrow Creek deal."

"You're the boss, Hoss." I pushed the limit with this reference, but didn't think he particularly cared. For all I knew he could've had the Cartwright gene. There was a vague similarity to the Bonanza character, the cowboy star. Gates was large-bodied with reddish-blonde hair. He sometimes wore his cowboy hat with pressed jeans covering the tops of dark brown cowboy boots, and appeared to have done some hard labor.

Another insight Jim Tucker told me was Gates had never formally trained in newspapering, but inherited the business from his father, who had died suddenly of a heart attack a few years back. Apparently he was the only heir and in need of a career.

In hindsight, there was a sense of relief Jen turned down dinner.

As the day dragged on, I eventually managed a pile of press releases. Ninety-nine percent didn't have any relevance to the community. Yet it was mystifying how much mail was coming from all over the country. Between mail, emails and the wire service, it was easy to spend half the day catching up on the daily grind of the American enterprise. An example was: 'Lifestyle Choices Can Help Animals Live Longer' from an animal rights group, offering an animal-friendly recipe for tofu. This was not suited for Great Valley though, as it was one of the top hunting spots in the world, cattle country and a place where people fished a lot. Here it was people rights, and animals were preserved for the dinner table.

In the waning afternoon hours the office became increasingly hot. I mulled over what I thought Banyan's group would oppose besides the Sorrow Creek development. I was sure they would fight the gambling initiative as well, but they had said little publicly about the ballot proposal. So it was a chance to make contact. I tried calling Blanche Banyan, happy to get voice mail since it gave me an excuse to visit Banyan's spread.

The Banyan ranch wasn't the place to show up unexpectedly, but there was an open gate across a gravel lane leading to the compound. I decided to risk it by driving down a cottonwood-lined road toward the gigantic lodge that Derrick Banyan once called home. Shaded areas along the esplanade surrounded the log mansion. Further to the south was a large concrete tarmac area in front of a six-car garage where two late-model pickup trucks and a red Blazer were parked. It was my lucky day, I thought.

I walked up wooden steps, onto the covered porch that seemed to stretch south all the way to New Mexico and north to Wyoming. For a tree-hugger, Banyan had done a good job of preserving an entire forest with redwood stain.

My footsteps sounded hollow against the boards, almost like the ghost of Derrick Banyan marching in the direction of the massive hand-hewn front door with beveled panels. I stuffed my pen and notebook into my back pocket, so as not to appear too anxious for information.

As I reached the door, it opened, and Blanche Banyan appeared in the log frame. Blanche was rather tall and stocky, sporting a bushy haircut. Although she was as far from being a local as Siberia was from the Sahara, she was aggressively involved in certain facets of the community. Her climb to the top of Great Valley's social register was the Greater Valley Fire and Ambulance Protection District as *the* top paramedic.

"Hi, Blanche," I said and immediately followed with, "I tried calling before I came but no one answered."

"Hello." She grimaced slightly at the intrusion. "What can I do for you, Spiver?" She and her colleagues seemed to have acquired a distaste for the *Great Valley Beacon*, judging by the rapid decline in communication between us. After the funeral, the Red River Coalition had gone into a torpid state, which I mistook as mourning.

"I was in the neighborhood and wanted to check on whether you had an opinion on the gambling initiative. We're doing a special election section and I could use some quotes."

"What's so special about it?"

"You might be in it."

"I doubt it since we haven't prepared a statement on any impact it might have."

"Should I call you later?" I wanted to keep the door open.

"That'd be a good idea," she said. "Next time you need to get permission before entering. We okay on that?"

"Oh sure, sorry." I smiled, and began to turn around to retrace my steps when she added: "So how are things at the paper? Slow news day — is that what really brings you out this way?" She had been helpful earlier in providing a lot of background information on Banyan, but was somewhat frigid today, until her curiosity showed up.

"Things are starting to pick up since the gambling initiative. But I'd like to do a story on what's going to happen with the coalition now that Derrick is no longer around."

It was an attempt at another angle. Not surprisingly, she seemed agitated by the remark and snapped back with: "We're regrouping. I'll let you know how it turns out."

I had driven by the ranch a couple of times before Banyan's death. Rarely was there any activity except for a foreman and his crew working cattle in the fields. Yet, with Banyan now gone, there was more action, judging by the late model cars and trucks parked in the drive.

Next stop was home, where I thought Lucy would be waiting with open arms, or at least the open files with registration cards in them. I parked in front and went into the lobby where Eloy still perched at the counter. "Hi," I said and walked toward the desk.

He stared at my entrance, as if telling me not to bother. "She ain't here. Gave her the night off, thinking she needs a break after working all day."

9

A week later I still hadn't seen Lucy around the motel. At first I figured Eloy Munn must have changed her schedule to strictly days from nine to four, about the only time I couldn't go home unless it was an emergency. And even then it was almost impossible the way Jen was always pressing for more stories, especially on deadline.

And I still didn't have anything concrete from Blanche Banyan's camp, so my news stories took on the mundane life of a small town that settled like cement in Rusty Gates' craw.

Suddenly Rusty ranted at one of our editorial meetings, "What's with these stories we're running on city council projects and the school board meeting?"

"What can I say, it's part of the job."

"Well, they've bogged down the action. Get off your butt. I want to breathe some life into this paper before it stinks of boredom."

"We're saving all the good stuff for the special election section," I lied. "Remember?"

"All I've seen are profiles of some of the players, like you got'm off press releases." That part was true, when he referred to all the local politicians and pro-business types supporting the gaming initiative. But it was work tracking these people down and doing interviews with the same like minds all day, and yet still keep up the daily grind with all the other news stories, which multiplied at an alarming rate.

Before I had a chance to ask him why he was in left field, Jeannette got us back on track. "How about a spread on the Sorrow Creek project. Starting with the history of the basin and its future prospects?" An overlay of sorts, she explained, which included Omni's abandoned oil shale project, a massive tract of land stripped bare of vegetation and wildlife for roads and the shale processing plant and refinery. She had made the suggestion at our usual meeting place, Joe's Doughnut Hut, across the street.

We were sitting in a booth, sipping coffee and discussing what the paper was lacking. Eating breakfast at Joe's was a weekly ritual that served as our conference on current affairs.

Our meeting took place in the dingy side room off the main dining area, where Jeannette laid out the week's game plan regarding the Sorrow Creek project. In turn, Jim and I fed her story ideas. Rusty would give his approval, nod or not.

Everyone agreed with Jeannette. Tucker would shoot the photos. I would do the story. Rusty sat quietly, taking it all in with a blank expression.

Jim Tucker and I worked well together. Although we had our differences of opinion, Rusty Gates and I basically respected each other. And of

109

course, I got along well with Jen. At the time I considered the three of them my closest friends in Great Valley. However, Lucy at the Lucky U would eventually make it to the top of the list.

Jen's assignment got us out of the office and off the phones for a day. Tucker's eye for photography always complemented the stories we ran, plugging about fifty percent of the pages in the *Beacon*.

That afternoon we drove up above the Sorrow Creek Basin on a dry, dusty road that climbed radically with huge ruts that tore hell out of the undercarriage. It was a relatively calm day with a bright sun. Below, the tall spindly cottonwoods along Sorrow Creek had a green sheen that shimmered in the slight breeze. Cows and horses grazed on small patches of green in the brownish desert-like fields. We bounced along in the Trans Am for about an hour until hitting a gate and, almost, a grizzly looking guy that was holding up his hand in the halt position.

"You fellows need approval to go any further," said the husky guard after we told him we were there to do a photo shoot for the paper. Although Omni's oil shale operation had been abandoned for several years, it was still well protected. Getting authorization would be nearly impossible.

When the old buzzard retreated into his shack, Tucker got out of the car and began snapping pictures of the gate and the signs threatening prosecution for trespassing. This brought the guy leaping out of his dwelling, yelling, "If you boys ain't pointed back down that road in two seconds, it'll be the sheriff doing the picture taking and them photos ain't going to be a pretty sight. Now git your asses out of here."

Breaking the law as a journalist wasn't something I was used to, but then again it wasn't unfamiliar territory either.

On the way back to the office I confessed to my first encounter to the Tuck man. It had occurred at the *Vegas Vanity*, where I had helped circulate the magazine. Tucker perked up from his half-slumped position against the door as he tried to cool off.

"How come the AC doesn't work? Now I have to roll up the window to hear this," he complained, but his interest was clearly piqued.

I ignored his question and the discomfort of the stifling car. "I'd drive around town, dropping off large bundles of slick rag to nudie joints, sex shops and street bums, who passed them to tourists along the Strip and in front of downtown casinos."

"So what were you guilty of, perversion?"

"There weren't any charges, but the delivery job had certain consequences to it, like the possibility of jail time for solicitation of pornography. The publisher always told me not to worry about the cops because there was a bail fund.

"Of course he wasn't serious, nobody in town bothered Rudy Morris, with his thinly veiled ads offering prostitution in the guise of escort services, massage therapists, or live models. Morris believed that to sustain a profitable publishing operation in a town where reading had a low priority there had to be strong sexual enticements with memorable photos."

When we got back to the office, Tucker disappeared down the hall toward the rear of the building where the production area was located. A halfhour later he arrived at my desk with what few pictures he had printed of the gate and guard shack. I thought they epitomized what I was up against in getting a decent story.

One of the pictures was of the gruff old man, pumped up, in a blue uniform and baseball cap, pointing his finger at the camera. It had captured the essence of rage. Even behind the guard's dark aviator glasses you could sense anger in his eyes and contorted, weathered face. But that was to be expected, since Omni probably didn't have any problem finding the roughest bulldogs in the security guard pound.

I ran the picture by Rusty and asked him, somewhat jokingly, if that's what he had in mind. He didn't laugh but stared, wheels turning in his head like a Sherman tank grinding along its track. "Look in the archives for some old aerials of Sorrow Creek during the oil shale days. We can start there and work our way to the future," he finally said. "Research everything, starting from the beginning of Omni's presence in the valley. I think we need to be looking at more than just a developer's dreams."

I was skeptical of his intentions, or unsure if he knew what angle he wanted to achieve. "Got anything specific you want me to explore?"

"I'm leaving that in your capable hands." He handed back the photo of the crusty geezer. "Here, this should provide some inspiration."

* * *

With each subsequent trip through the archives I paid more attention to details. Several times I found Derrick Banyan's name linked in some way with various energy projects around the region. There were several stories where he accurately predicted the consequences of a gas company's detonating an atomic bomb underground in hopes of unsealing the deep pockets of natural gas around Great Valley.

"Operation Plowshare" was part of the federal government's idea of promoting peaceful uses for atomic energy. So an energy company detonated a 42-kiloton bomb, about the size of three Hiroshima bombs, eight and a half miles down under. At the time, Banyan had claimed there was a strong possibility of radiation contaminating future natural gas wells after the explosion. "But did they listen?" asked Banyan rhetorically, in a story written after the fact that the 455 million cubic feet of natural gas underground once released would be worthless. And maybe even be poisonous to the ground water.

However, the venture benefited Great Valley Ready-Mix Co., which sealed all the wells with more concrete than it took to build a fifty-mile stretch of highway.

It was beginning to look like Banyan and his coalition were a mild version of the early '70s eco-terrorist movement. A period Edward Abbey fictionalized with 'radicals' who went around burning billboards, blowing up dams, sabotaging coal trains and sweetening construction equipment with sugar. However, Banyan fought his battles with

113

threats of lawsuits and a barrage of press releases, all the while lobbying legislators.

I broke the Sorrow Creek feature into three pieces. Part one consisted of revisiting the boom-and-bust cycle of the oil shale industry and Omni's role in it. Part two was a look at the future of the pristine valley and what we guessed was possibly next on the horizon – something only a press release could describe elegantly: Urban Sprawl. And finally, there was the piece I did about Halcyon Industries, an offshore oil service contractor headquartered in the Caribbean.

The archives on Halcyon were thick as Texas crude. Its local impact on the economy was sizeable. Halcyon was the main contractor that was in the process of developing the infrastructure for Omni's oil shale operations before the bust. During both companies' stints in Great Valley, unemployment dipped to an all-time low, while filling the county coffers to an all-time high. As Great Valley prospered, so did every offshoot of commerce, mainly the realtors, bankers, bar and liquor store owners. Even *The Beacon* had a stake in its prosperity by selling more subscriptions and ads.

And yet Halcyon didn't have a good track record with the local press. The company had persuaded a U.S. magistrate to rule that the paper turn over all the negatives of unpublished photos of the wastewater Halcyon pumped into Sorrow Creek. In the lawsuit, property owners – organized by Banyan's coalition – had unsuccessfully sought damages for groundwater pollution allegedly caused by Halcyon. The commissioners backed Halcyon throughout the ordeal and then awarded it several bids to build two schools, a large public works plant and a community center.

It was past history that worked well in the present. And it was the foundation for the series Rusty Gates approved of, beginning with the next commissioners' meeting.

Rusty Gates stared contentedly at the front page spread on his desk. The two of us discussed the main stories that were topics at the meeting. "So last night you were able to confirm that Halcyon is the construction firm selected to build the Sorrow Creek project?" He lit a cigarette then reclined back in his soft leather chair, resting his boots on the desktop. "That just smacks of coincidence, doesn't it?"

I said, "You mean that Halcyon gets all the large scale contracts and middles the rest to the locals?"

"That's why the rich get richer and the locals get the crumbs. But as long as everybody gets a piece of the pie, who's complaining. It wouldn't hurt if we got some of that action. All those casino and hotel ads, restaurants, you name it. Let's put a positive spin on it, Spiver. You might even get that raise I promised you after the thirty-day probationary period." He laughed, then took a puff, exhaling the blue cloud slowly. "When exactly did you start?"

"It's been well over a month," I said.

He ignored that, so I did as well. But it made me wonder how Banyan would have reacted to that way of thinking while I tried not to wheeze from all the smoke he was blowing in my direction that wasn't just from a Camel.

115

"So you like that Omni and Saville's company have more in common than just water rights, land leases and all three of the commissioners' blessings."

Rusty smiled. "Yeah, it's golden. I'm guessing it's good Halcyon is still around".

You could almost see the gears of corruption moving in sync. Like an old pocket watch hanging by a gold chain from some oil baron.

When Derrick Banyan was alive he vehemently opposed the possible destruction of the Sorrow Creek Basin. But, at the latest commissioners' meeting, the opposition from Blanche and the Red River Coalition swirled like a weak twister at a reinforced infrastructure that wouldn't budge. For the last week and a half, nothing from the coalition was very newsworthy or noteworthy. At the latest meeting, Victor Saville predictably countered any objection by claiming he was open to compromise.

It was the same old stuff, except for the change in the commissioners' attitude when they announced Halcyon would be the main contractor for the lakefront community and golf resort. Their appreciation for Saville's corporation was the lead headline.

Gates leaned forward and squashed the cigarette butt into a Caesar's Palace ashtray he apparently had stolen from the Vegas hotel. He pulled open the side drawer and produced a bottle of Jack Daniels with two shot glasses, something he was prone to do occasionally during lunch breaks. "Well hell, this calls for a celebration. You want one?"

I wasn't sure what we were celebrating, but didn't care. "Sure, why not?"

He poured two shots, and before I had a chance to reach across the desk for mine, he had already downed his and started pouring another. "You know that contest we're running for a free trip to Laughlin?" he asked after swallowing his second.

"Sure. You mean where ten people will get a free charter plane ride to a casino for a night, compliments of you, the charter service and the hotel? But the lucky winners get stuck with the obligatory $500 buy-in."

He laughed. "When you put it that way, it sounds like a scam. No, it's legitimate. The buy-in is completely refundable. All they have to do is give it back at the end of their stay. Who knows, they could easily triple it, too. It's a hell of a deal, by the way. Anyway, I want you to do a feature on the winners. Tag along, so to speak. Take some pictures and do a couple of positive interviews. Think about it."

After spending nearly a lifetime in Nevada, I hadn't seen many winners, even if they were comp'd all the way there. Still I didn't need to think about it, but instead raised my shot glass in a toast to the future. "Let the chips fall like manna from heaven."

He said, "Look at it this way, the contest is a way of promoting Great Valley's future gambling prospects. Why don't you get on board with this?"

"You mean I'm not as excited as I should be about it?"

"It's not that. You *do* seem a little negative lately. Or maybe it's that you're not being objective enough when it comes to our best interests."

"Sure, your best interests. Got it." I said. "Twist things any way you want, it's your call. I'm just reporting what's there in front of me."

117

If both the leisure community and gambling came to fruition, it would be a huge boon to the local economy. The venerable Rusty Gates could fulfill any dreams of becoming a casino owner and selling home sites on the surrounding hills where the lake would be. "Great Valley is a lot more desirable than Laughlin," he said, as we lounged in his office sipping Jack.

"It's a great place," I agreed with a giddy alcohol buzz.

"Less hot and more of a sophisticated crowd here." He was comparing Great Valley's upstanding residents to Laughlin's transient population and those who lived across the border in Bullhead City. "Most of them drifters. Up to their eyeballs in debt and end up living across the Colorado River in that shanty town."

"Yeah, that won't happen here in Great Valley," I said.

After the last shot we had together, Rusty Gates told me that, *if* he had the right investor, he planned on being part of the building process in Great Valley. Like the guy whose name was something Laughlin. And that's why Victor Saville had sought out Rusty's help to "get things right" in the paper.

10

During the next week Gates became preoccupied with the gaming prospect and wanted editorials to focus on all of its angles.

Our little editorial staff discussed the possibilities of a thriving real estate market and land speculation, something that hadn't happened since the boom years of oil shale, or when Union Carbide had cranked out vanadium yellowcake for atomic bombs.

Other gambling issues we wanted to focus on included concerns about new facilities and services, and long-held family values. Some folks with outlying homesteads saw their acres as dollar signs while those in town, who had to contend with gambling pollution, were scared as hell by possible increases in taxes, crime and undesirable neighbors with all sorts of addictions.

Jen had asked me to write a column about the gambling initiative, "From the Eyes of a Gambler", which would come out for voters during the special election in next month. We were sitting at her desk discussing whether it would pass when she suggested the editorial.

"You're the one who should write on the evils of gambling since you are so familiar with them," she had commanded. Jen was adamantly against gambling and sure as hell didn't want it coming to her town.

I had to agree with her if I didn't want a fissure in our friendship. Nevertheless, I also knew she was right, only because my bets have never had a big payoff. I've never hit the jackpot, instead the elusive payoff had sucked me dry more than a few times.

"You make me sound like I came from hell or something," I said.

"Or Las Vegas."

"So you hold that against me?"

"No, no, it's a great place. Every town should strive to be like Vegas." Sarcasm had always been one of her endearing qualities.

"I'm proud of my heritage," I said, hoping to add levity to the situation.

"I have to admit, it's served you well."

"What do you mean?"

"You've made it all the way to the *Great Valley Beacon*."

Despite agreeing to write the editorial, I was mostly ambivalent about gambling, even though it was an inherent part of my family life. Early on, my overwhelming desire had been to be a professional gambler like my father, or at least a blackjack dealer. In my early twenties, I was so committed to gambling I hardly noticed that it had become the corrosive agent that rusted away parts of my life.

120

Instead of going to college, I ended up working for Rudy Morris's smut magazine and studying landing patterns of the little silver ball on the roulette wheel. I tracked kings, queens, jacks, and aces playing blackjack. I looked to my watch for lucky signals at a casino. Stupid and superstitious stuff like: if a clock read 12:34, I headed straight for a card table hoping for a straight. 3:21 I associated with a sports book deadline and the need to wager. That's a bit exaggerated, but to the point as well.

I couldn't help it. Numbers had always been a pervasive influence in my life. It was more about numerology than math or statistics. Once I strongly believed numbers had metaphysical properties, like bad luck being associated with thirteen.

Numerology had the same connection to arithmetic for me as astrology to astronomy; not unlike the relation luck had to gambling. Although seven had various meanings in craps, luck depended on the positioning of the player's chips, similar to where one's birthday fell on the astrological chart.

No matter what sign a person was born under it always paid to hedge your bet, to have some sort of counter balance, like completely ignoring the significance of any number or sign and just lay the bet down. Damn, if it didn't work some of the time.

Whatever it was that made gambling attractive, I knew I wasn't compromising my journalistic integrity by opposing it. An editorial piece could suggest its inherent risk to society as a whole. However, in reality I was a gambleholic, forever hoping to capitalize on a long shot while fighting off the urge and surge of desire to quit cold. And if writing an anti-gambling piece meant scoring points with Jeannette, the more the merrier. It opened with:

Hooked On Gambling

> Gambling has always been in my blood. Believe it or not, I'm in this world because of a chance encounter at a craps table. But it doesn't mean gambling and its consequences should be part of just any community. Games of chance are pervasive enough in life without having to seek out organized crime to be your neighbors.

I thought my column would get Jen's attention. And to counter the constant stream of pro-gambling editorials by Rusty, which could run under the generic headline of 'Everybody Benefits With a Casino In Town.'

"I can't wait much longer." She gripped the top of my shoulders with both hands, pushed down and lowered her body to get a better view of the computer screen. "How's it coming?" Her long hair was partially draping my head and face.

"That feels good." I sighed under the pressure of her deep tissue massage and the tickling sensation of her hair.

"What's this?" Jeannette howled with laughter. "You were born on of top a craps table?" She read aloud from the screen's display of the editorial.

"That's not what it says."

"Oh, conceived then?"

"Wrong again. Give me a few more minutes and you'll get the whole burrito." I leaned back in the

122

chair and craned toward the ceiling as she stood upright and crossed her arms.

"Hope it's worth it," she said, while her smile spread across my personal heaven. "I don't want to lose hope over some crap shoot I bet Rusty won't run." She laughed again. By the time I swiveled around in my chair she had walked away. I turned back to the text, deflated, but continued anyway:

> When I finally left Nevada, I was free from the influence of roulette, blackjack and craps. Keno cards were no longer on every restaurant table like another condiment. Gone were the lighted number boards against the walls I'd stare at while trying to digest a cheap steak and watered-down coffee.
>
> I had moved on, across several state lines that separated preoccupation with occupation. I had escaped the great American wasteland, or so I thought. When the proposed Great Valley gambling story broke, I started to wonder if the road I had taken wasn't just going in a big circle.
>
> Since I came from a family of gamblers there has always been an urge to risk it all with little or nothing to show afterwards.

The op-ed went on in the same vein. I included bits and pieces of how it all started when my parents met in Las Vegas. My father had enlisted in the Army Air Corps and had trained to be a pilot at the

Las Vegas Aerial Gunnery School. Meanwhile, my mother had left her family digs in Newark and gone west to work at Basic Magnesium, Inc. in Las Vegas, doing her part for the war effort – as she always emphasized during flashbacks of the more gratifying parts of our family history.

She was one of hundreds of women factory workers who assembled airplane components for BMI, which in turn shipped them to California airplane manufacturing plants like Boeing and Hughes.

According to my mother, who claimed to have the only clear recollection of the event, she and my father met at the El Rancho motel and casino when the Strip was known only as Highway 91. They became interested in each other across the green felt expanse of a craps table. My mother had won a lot of money. He had lost all of his. She loaned him some of her winnings for a late night meal of black coffee and scrambled eggs, and a motel room. Shortly after that they married Vegas-style. It took all of fifteen minutes. Then they were separated by the war. He went off to fly gunners in the South Pacific. When my father was discharged, we continued living in Las Vegas, even after my parents lost it all and became indentured to the very gambling industry that took their dignity, and then restored it as he worked up the ranks to become one of the top managers in town.

I didn't care how anyone analyzed the editorial. Whatever the outcome, I didn't have anything to lose that I hadn't already lost at some point before, like a job. And besides, I was used to being under the microscope, having looked up at the mirrored

124

ceilings and surveillance cameras every time I walked into a casino.

Needless to say, Rusty Gates was completely hacked off and said so after reading the piece while proofreading the editorial page in his office. "What the fuck is this all about," he said, lighting another cigarette. "I thought I made myself clear about the paper's stand."

"Sure, do what you want, but we're starting to look like those fake ads we've actually been paid to print. You know the ones with a disclaimer, pretending like it was a legit newspaper article. 'This is an advertisement only' in tiny print above the headline, intended to deceive readers as a promotional about how some bank is the world's leading authority in credit restoration."

He acted incredulous. "What you're saying is that the editorial page is nothing more than propaganda?"

"There's a lot of people in this town who think you're full of shit because they believe you might be in cahoots with the mob and are trying to sell the town short."

He frowned. "Short of what?

"It's real potential."

"Like another boom with oil shale or uranium. Hell, if you ask me, this seems like the perfect fit. Something all the miners and roughnecks would appreciate, a distraction from the work load. Living for a change in nice homes and condos with a resort and casino nearby. Don't forget, a lot of recreational potential, too. No, Spiver, I think you have it backwards." He laughed at that, but not for long.

"Besides, editorials are written to influence the public. So can that crap about your family history. No one cares about your past gambling problems except you and maybe Jen."

I left the little disagreement in Rusty's office behind me, sick of it and everything associated with gambling. As a distraction, I paid Tucker a visit at his desk to ask him if he had heard anything about Derrick Banyan's accident investigation, other than what I had gotten from the chief that seemed like ten years ago. Tucker had a lot of contacts and was a reliable source. But he didn't tell me anything new. And so far the cops hadn't done much beyond the initial report.

As we talked, Rusty Gates blew by us and scurried out the door wearing his white cowboy hat. That ended our conversation about Banyan.

"Where do you suppose Rusty's off to in such a hurry?" I asked.

"I think he's got some friends flying in from Laughlin, the ones who own the charter service in Crescent City, and is probably late meeting them," said Tucker. Then he wondered aloud, "You think that contest is going to do anything for us?"

"If nothing else, it'll draw a lot of attention. Doesn't everybody want a free trip to Laughlin? And besides, it's got to be more exciting than those gambling stories we've been running. No offense," I said.

"None taken," he said. "Especially considering more than half of those stories are yours." Tucker was right. I usually got stuck with the main stories Gates wanted covered, no matter if they were insipidly inspired. But it wasn't anyone's fault.

Generally everyone agreed to a lack of investigative coverage.

No wonder we needed contests.

11

"Gates wants me to go to Laughlin, do some features on the winners of the contest," I was telling Jim Tucker after I had finished meeting with Rusty Gates in his office.

The only thing Tuck said was, "Sounds like the perfect assignment."

"I could include some of the vagaries of a gambling town to keep it interesting. It might be the only way back to my reporter roots," I said.

Tucker knew my newspaper career began at a Las Vegas magazine. My first assignment had been operator of an immense black Mergenthaler Linotype machine in the advertising department of *Vegas Vanity*. It forged lines of type with small, letter-shaped molds; little bricks of words which made up part of the magazine's money stream. I had written paragraph-long bios for various call-girl ads and brothels outside Pahrump in neighboring Nye County. Stuff like: "Call Flower with a fabulous, fantastic and fascinating figure! Learn more about this former teacher who performs a class act . . ."

128

The budding career of a journalist.

"Secretly, you really do want to go to Laughlin, don't you?" Tucker asked. "Even if everything was free, I'd be hard pressed to spend a weekend flying across the desert to a town full of casinos with a bunch of losers."

"That's not fair. They won a trip to the land where anything is possible." I had no idea what an understatement that was at the time.

Laughlin, ninety miles north of Las Vegas, didn't exist when I was growing up. Laughlin came of age during the '70s and was named by the man who created it, Don Laughlin. It rose out of the hot sandy Sonoran bluffs along the Colorado River with the sole purpose of servicing frugal gamblers unable to afford all the indulgences of Vegas. Not exactly a glimmering oasis, but more like a sweltering desert community during the day that sparkled like a small cluster of rhinestones at night.

"You know, Tuck, Laughlin once had the reputation of a place where people came to retire from life, eventually by cardiac arrest from pulling nickel slots, or a self-inflicted gunshot wound. Take your pick."

"What the hell's that supposed to mean, Wily?"

"You don't remember reading about the chief prosecutor of Dade County, Florida who came to Laughlin to retire?"

"That was way before my time, you old coot."

"Watch yourself, Tuck, I'm not that much older than you," I said, not wanting to admit I had about seven years on him.

"What's this, another bullshit story about the good old days where some guy hits the jackpot and lives out his days in the life of luxury? Might as well save the fluff piece Rusty's going to want you to write as a contest promotional," said Tuck.

"Yeah, that's a good angle," I said sarcastically. "But the guy lasted less than two days before killing himself, saving the swat team outside his hotel room the trouble."

That got Tuck's attention. "Okay, that's more like it. And better than I imagined for a sidebar describing Laughlin's clientele."

I explained in more detail. "If this prosecutor thought a person was guilty he'd make sure of it by planting evidence, and as a matter of course, seize everything that person owned. The jury found the guy guilty on thirty counts with things like abuse of office and conspiracy. He fled to Laughlin probably thinking he could blend in."

"Why don't you add that to your list of story ideas? Jen'd love it."

"When I told Rusty during our little get-together he gave me that stare of his. You know the one: 'Why the fuck do I want to know all this?' look."

Laughlin fit Rusty Gates' personality like a lambskin condom. To me, Rusty was a small-time operator with a flamboyant attitude who stayed and played under a circus tent with his harem. I came to find out he knew all sorts of women, some of them from various parts of Nevada.

I found it distressing and frustrating at times, but working for Rusty Gates was a cakewalk, overall. Until gradually everything took on a darker side.

Although Gates was a likeable enough guy, he seemed preoccupied with every potential capital venture project that came down the pike. He was given to bouts of writing editorials that went beyond the mainstream of the community's conservative boundaries, like the idea of wanting to turn Great Valley into a gambling Mecca. His tabloid-style headlines claimed: "Real Estate Speculators Say Time Has Come" or "Future Depends on Voter Approval" and "Many Stake Claim on Positive Prospects". All the while he failed to mention anything negative.

Then his shady business deals also started to come into focus.

Meanwhile, stories about the continuing investigation of Banyan's death missed the target too. It wasn't a lack of effort to uncover the truth, but the inability to get past the gambling issues that made up all the front-page news. But then again, the paper hadn't received any pressure from Blanche Banyan's camp as to why we weren't running any more stories on the car accident. It was turning into an unsolved mystery.

At an impromptu editorial meeting with Jen, I told her we needed an article on the police investigation into Banyan's accident. She agreed, but only if there was something to report.

The chief wasn't responding well to my questions after a brief conversation over the phone. However, when pressed, he responded with, "We're looking into it. We have something to go on you'll be the first reporter I'll call."

"One last question before you hang up? Could Banyan's death possibly be a homicide?" Whatever the answer, I wanted it to lead off in my next story.

131

"I'll let you know, Spiver. But until then I would keep that theory under wraps."

With that lack of information I headed home for the day.

I pulled up to a biker in the parking lot out front of the motel and got out. He ignored me, too busy running his hands through his long raven hair and cleaning his bushy mustache of bugs.

Before he had a chance to acknowledge me, I grabbed my six-pack off the seat and walked toward the lobby. Lucy was perched on a high stool watching TV behind the counter. She smiled when I came through the front door. It was around seven; soon things would start picking up in the motel world, road warriors pulling off the highway for the first available room.

"Long time, no see," I said. "I thought you were avoiding me for some reason. And I didn't know why. You never called or left a note. But, I have a feeling you thought Jen and I had something going."

"I wouldn't try to control who you date or why. Munn fired me. Thought we were doing the hanky panky when he wasn't looking. That's what he called it, hanky panky. Can you believe it? Anyway, the guy who took my place took off leaving Munn in a fit."

"That sort of explains it. But no contact?"

"First he banned me from the place and now I'm supposed to work the busy times until he relieves me, or finds somebody else. And since it's coming up on the weekend I'll be swamped for awhile."

Most of Munn's guests ended up at the Lucky U because of its convenience to the highway population looking for a good deal. In Great Valley all motel

132

owners conspired to charge the same price: the only difference was location.

One thing Eloy Munn couldn't be accused of was violating the Federal Fair Housing Law, which prohibits discriminating against anyone. Everyone was welcome at the Lucky U as long as they paid in advance.

Walking in behind me was the large rugged-looking guy draped in black leathers wanting a room for the night. At first I suspected Lucy's smile was for him, not me, and I planned on coasting through the lobby without saying much, thinking she wanted to flirt with him. The guy must have been about six-three with his big mop of hair and thick-soled boots. A Mad Max look, starring this Mel Gibson look-alike.

But she stopped me cold with, "Wily, when you have time we need to talk. Your door was partly open, and I was wondering if you were expecting guests."

The biker leaned into the counter, scribbling on the registration card Lucy had furnished him. He stared at me hard until he turned to concentrate on Lucy's good looks.

"I'll stop by later," I said and walked to the bottom of the stairs, concerned there were bigger problems waiting in my room.

"Let me know in a while how things turn out." She had become harried and anxious to get rid of the guy who claimed to be driver's license-less.

"Look, I don't give out my ID for anybody. Nothing personal," said the biker when Lucy had asked for it. She charged him twenty bucks more than the posted rate. When he complained, she

133

snapped back that it was policy without any form of identification.

I moved a step or two up the stairs and then stopped to see if there would be any trouble with the biker. But he just smiled and demanded the room key after paying with a hundred dollar bill, then headed out the door toward the parking lot.

The roar was deafening from the open throttle of his bike, reverberation echoing in the asphalt courtyard. The lobby's swinging glass doors rattled from the force. Once in gear, the bike lugged off toward the far end of the building.

"Someone might have broken into your room," Lucy said after the biker was well out of earshot. "But I couldn't tell, so I didn't want to call the cops until you arrived. The door was practically wide open. I closed it, though, and locked it." Then the registration card distracted her. Most of her black hair was pinned behind her ears but a few thick stands hung to the left of her furrowed forehead as she tried to make out the scribbles on the card.

"Who is it?" I asked, walking back toward the counter.

"I don't know. I can barely read the damn card."

I studied the top line for anything resembling a name, and vaguely made out something like 'Dick Suckler' scrawled in piss-room font. "I think it's some kind of message."

"Screw that dirt bag. I oughta call the cops for sexual harassment," she said. "Eloy would've . . . I'll probably get in trouble for letting him stay. But he was cute in his outfit. Sort of reminds me of, what's-his-name …? "

"Mel Gibson?"

134

"The gladiator, Russell Crowe."

"Now *I am* getting concerned about your taste in men," I said. "Did you see anything out of place when you closed the door?

"I didn't see anything disturbed that hadn't been disturbed before. If Munn hadn't fired me it would be a lot cleaner."

"I told Munn to tell the maid not to bother cleaning my room. By the way, thanks for not getting the cops involved."

"If the cops show up, it will probably be because they'll be looking for that greaseball." And she was absolutely right. However, her intuition was only one of her many endearing qualities.

As I was about to ask about the red Blazer, the phone rang. Lucy picked it up with her standard greeting: "Lucky U Motel, may I help you?" followed by a long pause, then: "Sure, I'll hold while you get your Visa."

"Lucy, I need a favor," I said. She was listening to the receiver, staring with disgruntled disbelief that she'd been put on hold for so long.

"Wily, you need to be stroking me more to come looking for favors," she said out of the corner of her mouth, still cradling the receiver with her left hand. "Yeah, I'm still holding," she said, muffling the receiver. "Can you believe they can't find the card after calling for a reservation?"

"I'd believe anything is possible in this world," I said and smiled. "But one thing for sure, you look absolutely fabulous."

"I don't care what Munn thinks, you're an okay guy. But if you're leading me on just to — yes, sir, I'm still here. You have the number?"

Mouthing the words, she confirmed the owner of the Blazer had checked out today. I suppose the phone was a distraction that prevented her from giving me a full tongue-lashing. "Could I put you on hold a moment? I have a call coming in on the other line." She cupped the receiver again and paused a moment. "I know we're both busy now, but maybe we could get together later."

"Sure. I better get to my room."

"Wait a sec," she said, but someone had drawn her attention back to the phone just as the glass doors swung open.

I whispered, "see you later" and she nodded with a smile.

As more guests began arriving, I didn't think Lucy would have any more problems with the biker. Little did I know there was a chance I might not ever see her again.

The saying "locks only keep honest people honest" would apply to the Lucky U Motel as long as the place remained standing. If a person pushed hard on a door, the jam would give enough to allow the dead bolt to slide out of its notch.

Motel break-ins happened, and sometimes without breaking in. If not a thief, it was the maid ransacking the place while cleaning up. A good motel motto was not to leave anything behind you didn't want others to find. In the battle of piracy vs. privacy, the odds were against anyone who thought their junk was untouchable.

There were few, if any, clues of a break-in. A couple of dirty shirts and jeans lay piled in a corner by the bed with a rumpled paisley spread on top. Old newspapers and pages of scribbled notes were scattered on the floor. The only evidence someone had stolen anything was the absent laptop, the most expensive single piece of equipment I owned.

I stared in disbelief at the sloppy and careless mess I created. I shuffled through the paper clutter over to the dresser. It appeared that nothing had been touched there, including the binoculars, which stood upright like two toy sentinels guarding the bureau. I said thanks and asked if the little troopers had seen anything suspicious. I picked up the black inanimate object, looking into the two big lenses resembling eyeglasses people wear in the final stages of sight, and wished I had seen first-hand the thief who would create chaos for the rest of my stay in Great Valley.

Faint voices were coming from the direction of the neighboring room. I listened intently, thinking there might have been witnesses. But maybe it was a den of thieves next door. Then I realized it was the clock radio on low volume. I had turned it down when Jen had called earlier that morning, but it felt like a lingering presence, or a clue about what would happen next. I was wrong.

Jeannette gave a quick rap on the partially open door of the motel room before peering in. "Has Eloy Munn been housecleaning again?" she said while surveying the dark cave-like dwelling for signs of life other than ourselves.

"Looks like a motel owner rifled the place, doesn't it?" I reached for the heavy motel curtains to pull them apart. Through the neglected grime and smoke-fogged window, I watched the sun setting behind the cliffs' shadow. There were a few more cars in the parking lot, including Jen's.

The room was hot, despite my having kept the drapes closed all day. For relief, I clicked on the AC and listened while it struggled to life. It awakened with a disgruntled whine, followed by several thunks of the fan whirling out of kilter. When it finally reached operating speed, the air filled with a mildew smell that could have croaked a cockroach.

"Pleasant isn't it? Reminds me what a tropical breeze would be like in Great Valley if the Caribbean Ocean were a few blocks away," said Jeannette, who continued to stand in the doorway.

"You're thinking Third World-ish?"

"It's like we're natives." She entered the room reluctantly, but then rolled onto the bed as if we were at the beach on holiday. Stretched out on her back, her chest rising with each breath, she added, "Ah, nothing like a romantic getaway."

"Shouldn't breathe so deeply, you could get Legionnaires' disease." I hoped it wasn't a joke that would come back later to haunt us.

"Close those drapes and come here," she said when I sat at the circular table, and on the perimeter of a dicey situation. Any moment Lucy Branch could show up. I figured the only reason she hadn't so far was the influx of guests at the front desk.

"I didn't have a chance to tell you yet, but I had a visitor earlier."

"Was it your personal maid, Lucy?" said Jen with a slight sneer starting to form on those voluptuous lips of hers. "I was just admiring the way she keeps things so tidy," she said, while laughing at the ceiling.

"No. It was an intruder who tore the place apart. And whoever it was took my computer for a walk." I

138

hoped to change the subject and her mood. Jealousy didn't become her. "You want to grab something to eat?"

I felt anxious and needed something to settle my stomach. As a partial cure, I reached for a bottle of scotch on the table and poured some into a clear plastic cup without ice. It was hot but soothing. Ice wasn't only a luxury in the Third World — it meant entering another realm, where Lucy worked in the motel's lobby.

Jen sat up on the edge of the bed. She watched the scotch slowly being drained from the cup. "How serious is it?" she asked. "I mean, what else did you lose?"

"They didn't take anything but the computer. And all the stories I've been working on. The ones I didn't send to you yet."

"How fast can you write?" she said half jokingly.

"Not fast enough to satisfy Rusty. I lost about five new stories and weeks of notes, especially on Banyan and the Sorrow Creek project."

"You didn't save anything?"

"I don't know, maybe my life by not being in the room when it was ransacked. The zip drives were in the computer case along with the laptop."

"And this really happened? You didn't just lose it in your car or at the office?" She gave me an oblique look. "Are you aware that your room always looks like it's been plundered?"

"It *really* happened, sure as you're lying on my bed," I said, but started to doubt whether I had actually left it in the room. Exact details sometimes eluded me, and at times I didn't really know why I had become a reporter when one of the most fundamental aspects of my job was flawed by my inability to thoroughly observe miniscule details. But from what I could determine, the computer with all its stories, and adventures, was the only thing missing.

The phone rang. It was Lucy calling from the front desk. Said she was on her way up. "Christ," I told her, "Not now. I'm busy and the place is a mess. Can I get back to you later?"

Jen was leaning up against the headboard, legs outstretched, listening to my side of the conversation. She knew it was Lucy before I had a chance to tell her. "She coming up?"

"Hope not," I said. "Don't really know. Anything's possible."

I reached to kiss her but she spontaneously jumped from the bed. "I'm out of here."

"I'll go with you."

"No." She snapped, then calmed down. "That's all right. Some other time, maybe."

"It's not what it looks like," I pleaded and got in front of the door to prevent her from leaving. But it didn't work.

"Then, fuck you anyway."

"That's not nice." I moved out of her way before there was a chance she would gore me with more of her quick retorts.

"What'd you expect, a quickie?" Jeannette demanded.

"No, but maybe a long-term romance, you think?"

"What good would that do? Keep your libido under control?" She stormed passed me and out of the room. I practically ran after her in a desperate attempt to stop her. "Let me explain, please," I yelled. She reached the stairwell, rapidly descended the steps, and flew out into the parking lot before I finally caught up with her flight to freedom.

"Jen, please," I repeated, as she was about to get into her Firebird.

She faced me for the first time since leaving my room. "Look, I'm not hanging around since you have other plans, that's all," she said. "I'll see you tomorrow at the office. I have to get home anyway."

"I'm telling you, I didn't have any plans . . . except with you." The last part was hard to get out, and I nearly choked on the lie. But it wasn't a lie. Or maybe it was. I had begun wondering how long I could avoid Lucy's unrelenting and seductive advances. I knew all too well the firm grip a particular vice had on me. "I meant . . . I just needed to talk to her about the person who drove the Blazer. That's all. It's vital to Banyan's story. Whoever rented the SUV is connected in some way to Banyan's death. I'm sure of it."

"And for no other reason? I find that hard to believe, Wily."

"It's true. There's too much between us to let the little things get in the way." And I firmly believed it at that moment.

"I've got to get going." And with that she got in the car and sped out of the parking lot, fast enough to draw everyone's attention.

12

There were about ten or twelve vehicles in the motel's parking lot, including the bike. The only one I cared about was my Trans Am. I got in, nearly dead from hunger, and headed to the Portal Bar.

Once there, I ordered a pizza. It was baked in a toaster oven at the bar. Only half was edible, any more would have put a person in an early grave. 'At least he didn't die of hunger' could have been etched on my tombstone. It was better than dying of boredom from filling out a report on a purloined computer, or languishing over other missing components of my life.

The Portal was half-empty. Those in attendance were mostly rednecks. I swiveled around on the barstool when a few local politicos rolled in shortly after nine. The one most recognizable was Blanche Banyan but I didn't care to acknowledge her in my dour state, so I turned around and watched in the mirror behind the bar as they sat at one of several open tables.

All three commissioners, including Blanche and another woman, sat at the round table. They had probably come from a meeting the press wasn't invited to. But the only feeling I had of being left out came from Jeannette's rejection.

A sweet bitterness burned inside me after taking a drink of cheap scotch until another gulp washed it away, along with any lingering taste of sausage and pepperoni. I suffered from heartburn, but it didn't come from pizza. I felt I wanted to hang on as long as possible to Jen, but it wasn't looking favorable to me.

Eventually my thoughts drifted along the bar to where one of the commissioners stood. Gus Ferguson was tall and rugged looking with limbs in direct proportion to his size. He wore a cowboy hat above a sculpted, red, weathered face. His eyes were disguised behind yellow-tinted aviator glasses. He waited for drinks from the bartender since there weren't cocktail waitresses in anyone's near future.

We exchanged greetings and small talk about whether the Sorrow Creek project or gambling would become a reality.

" . . . Or is it just another scheme to sell desert plots on the side of a cliff?" I said in all seriousness.

"That's real inter-resting, Spiver. We'll have to discuss your viewpoint further when it doesn't interfere with my social hour." He laughed, but quickly dropped any pretense of camaraderie when the drinks arrived.

The commissioner thanked Red, left a buck on the bar for a tip, and gave me a nod. I nodded back and smiled like we were old friends. He moseyed off toward his table to be with his real comrades. And I wondered if Blanche was one of them or the opponent. It seemed unlikely she would be hanging with them, but she was a rising political star since Derrick's death.

I sat alone and tried to be coy while studying them in the reflection and listening to the music. The jukebox was playing a country western song by Patsy Cline. Patsy's melodious voice in the hollow atmosphere felt like being alone on a dry windswept plain.

I took a sip of scotch to avoid choking up on the lyrics.

Through a misty fog the mirror took on the appearance of an Edward Hopper painting: A composition of nightlife in Great Valley depicting a lonely barroom. Dim lamps hung above tables while patrons hunched over their drinks, laughed or conversed within their circle. There were no defined corners in the mirror framed by shelves with bottles. Everything recessed into a hazy shadow, including the entrance, where a battered wooden door remained motionless despite my longing to see it open and Jen walk through.

But she didn't come.

I became bored with the whole scene, and depressed with an overwhelming sense of loneliness. Red was entertaining guests at the other end of the bar, so I skipped on any more drinks and decided to head home.

Parked under the yellow, incandescent streetlight outside the Portal was the red Blazer. I walked in its direction, and peered into the windows. On the passenger seat was a gray, pinstriped jacket and a leather satchel. The rental probably belonged to one of the women having cocktails with the commissioners.

Narrowing the origin of the red Blazer was tiring to pursue. And scotch made me careless, but I wandered back to the bar anyway. The two attractive women and the commissioners paid no attention to my entrance. Nor did anyone else as I sat at the bar and tried to order another drink. Red treated me as if I were a ghost from his past.

However, matching the sports jacket to a person's slacks proved easier than crawling under their table. I was saved the embarrassment when all five got up to leave. The woman wearing pinstripe pants and a blue blouse was lithe with cropped blonde hair and looked a lot like Blanche.

The significance of chasing the driver down was hard to justify since I didn't have a story to go with it. But what little research I had done couldn't be written off as another dead end. The car had appeared on numerous occasions by coincidence — at the hospital shortly before Banyan died, and later at his ranch. It was usually around when Victor Saville was staying at the motel. And finally, with the commissioners, the driver in broad bar light, stretching out her hand toward the smiling cowboy.

* * *

It was shortly past midnight by the time I got home. The room was hot, stuffy and gloomy. I stretched out on the bed in the dark and slipped into unconsciousness. Then the phone rang. And rang. I ignored the intrusion by burying my head in the pillow.

The phone rang again. It was an intoxicated Lucy wondering what had happened to me.

"Fell asleep," I told her.

"I tried calling earlier but you didn't answer. So were you with what's her name, Ms . . ." She paused in mid-sentence to add, "You there?"

"Didn't hear the phone in time. Sorry. You stop by a little while ago?"

"No, I don't think sooo." She giggled before letting out a screech, "Stop that!"

"What?" I asked. She had my curiosity up to an unexpected level that early in the morning.

"Oh, not you. This jerk here keeps trying to grope me. And it ain't happening."

She had company. Why was she calling? Was she teasing me? And was I falling for it?

"Who's your friend, the biker dude?"

"Yeah, and if he keeps getting fresh, you might have to save me!" She was tipsy and the dude was probably ready for action.

"Wily, come down and have a drink with us. Or we'll come up there."

"You never told me whose red Blazer that is."

"It's a secret I'll have to whisper'n your ear."

"I'm ready."

"No, dummy, your *ear*, not the *phone*." She giggled, somewhere between drunk and distracted. "We're coming up."

"Lucy, I'll be down shortly. Got to dress."

"Why?" she said and hung up.

I was really parched and headed to the bathroom. I stuck my head in the sink and took a sideways drink from the faucet. The warm mineral-tasting water forced me to spit more than swallow, but it cured a bad case of dry mouth. The thought of having to defend her against a biker made me want to puke. That and the water.

There was no need to search for a shirt and pants since I was fully clothed. But I stalled as long as possible, which meant nothing to Lucy because if I didn't go down she'd come up. I grabbed the scotch as a peace offering, but also as a Trojan bottle, for bashing the creep's skull. Fifteen minutes later and a couple cocktails alone, I headed toward the lobby.

She was asleep, resting her head on the sofa's armrest, frozen in time, like a statue grasping a Bud longneck. It was a disturbing sight, but one I could easily live with since the biker was no longer around. After the viewing, I took the bottle out of her hand and placed a cushion under her head, then sauntered back to a parched dreamscape.

I was awakened by muffled noises coming from the direction of the hall. The gruff voice was Eloy Munn, keys jangling in motion. In my drowsy state, I assumed he was opening up the adjoining room for a good cleaning. But Munn was questioning someone. A familiar voice responded. Keys rattled and the door handle moved slightly, and Munn's big round head popped in. It seemed he was as wide as he was tall. That was because he was bent over the door knob leaning half way into the room.

"Spiver, we're looking for Lucy," said Munn. "How come you didn't answer the door?"

"Didn't hear you knock." I said, quickly sitting up in bed, knowing that he hadn't bothered.

"Well, the police are here," Munn said and pulled the door closed, giving me a second to get out of bed before he let the cops in.

147

Using the line off an old TV show, I said, "What can I do for you, officers?" as they entered.

"Eloy claims his stepdaughter Lucy wasn't anywhere to be found when he came to work this morning and thought she might be with you," said Great Valley Police Department Lt. Joe Espanola. "Since no one answered your phone or door the first time Mr. Munn tried, he decided to call us." Munn might have been lying about that too.

"Don't you think Lucy's old enough to be on her own?" I asked Espanola.

"Last night's receipts are also missing," he explained wearily. I'd met Joe Espanola at the cop shop while picking up the police blotter. He was an old guy from a rural community in Utah. We had that in common; We'd both lived in Utah. He was Mormon, and once lived and worked up the road from the last place I was employed.

Joe Espanola stood next to my bed, watching me tie my shoes. I described the previous night's events to Joe and asked if they had checked the cocksucker's room Lucy had been with, the biker who had scribbled obscenities on the registration card.

"There wasn't any card like that or motorcycle in the parking lot," said Munn. "What room was he checked into?"

"I don't know."

Munn's beady-eyed stare was unwavering as he stood next to the door, behind a guy named Tim Summers, the other cop, who had been blatantly checking out my room. "The cash register was completely cleaned out," Munn blurted, getting to the heart of what really troubled him. "Know anything about that?"

"Only that he probably took advantage of Lucy," I said, hoping to protect Lucy from her stepfather's wrath. "That son-of-a-bitch probably took off with the money and Lucy too."

"You think he kidnapped her?" asked Munn, who stood menacingly above me as I struggled to my feet in an attempt to reach eye level.

"Wouldn't put it past the slime ball," I said, cross at the whole situation. I was having a hard time believing Lucy was the type of girl to be hanging with a biker, much less stealing anything from anyone, even Munn, though I'm sure he was substantially underpaying her.

Munn turned to the cop. "What do you think, Joe?"

"We need more evidence than the fact she's gone. Someone else might have taken the money," Espanola politely explained.

"More evidence, like what?" he demanded, then softened a bit by adding, "I'll admit she isn't someone to do such a thing. I've never had any trouble with her. In fact I've always trusted her most. Except my wife, of course. But evidence . . ."

"Like a ransom note," said Tim Summers, who palmed his bully club attached to the thick black belt that also supported a gun, radio, mace, bullets and a fat gut.

"Wait a minute, now, it's still early. She still might show up. Could she have gone for breakfast or taken the deposits to the bank?" asked Lt. Joe Espanola."

"I do that," said an angry Attila the Munn.

149

No one said anything, but it was obvious Munn was miffed that his stepdaughter might have ridden off on a hog with all the money, and there was little he could do except file charges against his own family member.

In an agitated voice Munn shifted the blame game by asking when my room had been broken into. "Why didn't you report it to me and the police?"

"Nothing was taken except a laptop, which was probably lost in a paper pile at the office," I said in a state of denial. I didn't want to report it stolen. If by some miracle the computer was found, it might have been held as evidence in an unsolved crime.

The cops told Munn not much could be done except to put out an all-points bulletin for Lucy and her "friend." In which case Lucy would probably be arrested as an accomplice.

What a lovely time for all, I thought.

"In the meantime," Espanola told me, "why don't you stop by the station so we can do an official report on the break-in of your room."

"What if I misplaced it?"

"Then we'll look in the lost and found. At any rate, Eloy noticed the door had been tampered with when he was making his maintenance rounds."

"How often is that, Eloy?" I said. "I didn't know you were into maintenance around here."

"Smart ass," he said. "You're beginning to piss me off, Spiver. Remember, I reserve the right to give you the boot whenever I feel. You're on notice."

If a small town is compared to living in a fishbowl, then living at the Lucky U would be Munn in the bowl with you, where he could zoom in on everyone's activities. It was obvious the invasion of privacy stretched further than eavesdropping on the phone lines.

Jeannette called shortly after the cops left. Her voice was as refreshing as a glass of Florida sunshine without the pulp friction. "Where were you last night? I tried calling," she said cheerily. "I'm sorry I acted so terrible. I was wrong to walk out in such a huff." She sounded so sweet and delightful I didn't want to ruin it all with the lurid details.

"Went to the Portal for a quick pizza and then fell into a deep sleep before getting caught in a Dragnet episode." I meant it in a lighthearted manner, but she took it so seriously that I regretted saying anything. And yet there was no way to hide the facts. I'd be writing up a story about it in the next edition.

"What's that supposed to mean, Sergeant Friday? You have delusions about your partner in crime?"

"Eloy Munn suspects Lucy and a biker might have run off with the motel's money. They thought I was somehow tied in with their disappearance." I was looking for a little sympathy, but all I got in return was skepticism.

"No wonder you didn't answer," Jeannette said.

"I never heard the phone." There was dead silence on the other end until I broke it with, "By the way, you're the last person I would have expected to call since you usually have other commitments that time of night." There was another long pause before I filled in the void with: "I missed you, though."

151

She seemed to ignore the last statement or didn't care. "I told Rusty about what happened to your computer. He wasn't all that worried about the missing stories. Says you can handle it. But he wanted to know how fast you can get everything you got together. In other words, when are you coming in?"

I said, "Soon. Sorry about missing your call."

"You mean that?" She sounded skeptical.

"Of course."

A place like the Lucky U can trigger distorted perceptions because of the emptiness that accompanies life in a dingy motel room. When I heard movement in the hall I hoped it was Lucy coming to save me from drowning in self-pity, so I opened the door to wishes and dreams.

Instead, Victor Saville was bounding down the hall in my direction. He approached, extending a fist then pointing his index finger at me. Saville wanted to know what the hell I was thinking. "Writing a fucking story that Banyan's death could have been murder," he huffed.

I had no idea where he was coming from. At first nothing connected. There hadn't been any stories that indicated Saville was behind his accident in the paper, except what I had stored in the laptop. Like a wild dog about to sink its teeth into flesh, he ripped into me again with his tirade.

"You know how much trouble you'll cause your family if a story defaming my organization got out?" He barked like a rabid dog let out of his cage. "And you got no idea what will happen to you, too."

"Why don't you make it clear for me what you're talking about?" I said with resolve and the need to shake him off. "I'm on my way out, if you don't mind."

"Think in terms of a personal loss." Saville hissed and slithered about like a snake ready to strike its prey and swallow it whole.

He finally rattled my brain enough into thinking he had committed the break-in. "Didn't know I was missing anything."

"Take a stroll down memory lane and you'll find it in a dumpster."

"So that's where I left the laptop."

"Along with other objectionable shit."

"So you got more than a sneak's peak. Whatever you found so gripping is only a rough draft. Notes to myself. Besides, everybody has a theory about Banyan's accident."

"Yeah, but yours are slanderous and in need of rectifying." Victor Saville wasn't the kind to joke around, and if he had his way it wouldn't be a stand-up routine. Instead I'd be lying in some grave. "It ain't my place to tell you how to do your job, but if I read anything in that goddamn paper insinuating that I had anything to do with Banyan other than a meeting, you're history, Spiver."

He stared so long and hard at me I had no choice but to take him at face value. But it wasn't Saville's threats that impeded progress. Instead I had become my own worst enemy since I considered Slick Vic might actually be telling the truth. I finally said, to break the tension, "Any chance of getting the thing back?"

"Whatever you're talking about doesn't exist," he said flatly. He turned around and walked a few steps toward the stairs, then turned again. With his spit practically landing on my shoe, he added: "You know, if it weren't for your family connections, there wouldn't be anybody around to discuss this with."

13

After Saville left there was the usual bitterness and resentment toward fate when it worked against my favor. In the old days I'd look to the casinos to ward off possible disaster. But instead of a winning hand I was dealt with a mountain of debt. By then the only escape from gambling was to seek solace in a newspaper position away from the glitter and litter, where the daily routine of working as a reporter kept the addiction in remission.

Of course there were better ways of making a living, like working on a gas rig in the vast desolation of the southwest. But I didn't want to settle for a job where the risks of physical pain outweighed any personal gain. However, I came to find out after working at the *Great Valley Beacon*, it's a fallacy to think there is a safe haven whether one is exposed to the elements of unnatural disasters or the unpredictable behavior of the human spirit.

I walked into the office hoping to get past the previous night, but found it difficult to concentrate on working in the stuffy atmosphere.

Jim Tucker was on assignment. Rusty and Jeannette were engaged in some kind of editorial discussion at her desk. I joined the group, and told them I was in search of a good solid story about Derrick Banyan's death because of a gut feeling. I didn't tell them that covering a land speculators' wet dreams had become a lifeless event where tedium was the overall theme. The Sorrow Creek project was moving slower than a Kansas avalanche.

I said, "Let's put the cops on the spot about why they haven't closed the Banyan case. That'll stir up some excitement."

"Sure," said Rusty. "Just keep the gambling initiative and Sorrow Creek project front and central."

Chief Higgins granted me a brief interview on the state of Banyan's case.

"Don't get your hopes up Spiver, I already told you everything there is so it shouldn't come as a surprise that we're closing the case on Banyan." The chief seemed wearied by my presence. And despite his reluctance to say much more than that, he managed a few more words, which resulted in:

Police Chief Closes Case On Banyan Accident

Great Valley Chief of Police Tom Higgins has officially closed the department's case in the death of prominent environmentalist Derrick Banyan.

The investigation concluded Thursday after Higgins and his department determined there wasn't any foul play in the rollover car accident, which took the life of Banyan.

"After reviewing all the circumstances surrounding the accident, we have determined Derrick Banyan fell asleep at the wheel of his Jeep Cherokee," said Higgins, adding that the results from the autopsy proved inconclusive. "There really is nothing new to report as of now."

Controversy has surrounded the incident from the very beginning. Banyan's Red River Coalition had claimed police were slow to react and never followed up on several tips that could have shed more light on the investigation. According to coalition spokesperson and Derrick Banyan's widow, Blanche Banyan, he had received several anonymous threats for his tough stand on various environmental issues throughout his career.

Two nights before his death, police issued a 'disturbing the peace' warning to Banyan and Victor Saville, the Las Vegas developer proposing the Sorrow Creek project. Allegedly, the two had been arguing in the parking lot of the Lucky U Motel.

Blanche Banyan didn't comment on any specific incident prior to his death, but thanked the Great Valley

Police. "I want them to know that Chief Higgins and his officers' time and energy while conducting the extensive investigation was greatly appreciated. Now that we know what caused the tragic accident, we can move on with other more pressing issues, which Derrick would have wanted." However when pressed, she would not elaborate on what those other issues are, except to forge ahead with efforts to reestablish the coalition's mission and goals in the upcoming months.

And that was that. It seemed over at that point, everything locked into place, and yet there wasn't anything in the chamber. Or it was a dud, placed there by an inertia so great and superficial there wasn't anything left to do, except drive by the Banyan ranch a couple of times to observe any changes that might have taken place.

There wasn't much time to search for clues in Banyan's death that were part of a solid story angle. So to expedite matters, I drove the Black Shadow down the ranch driveway. When I pulled up, Blanche Banyan was in the shady lane talking to the ranch foreman. I waved and she returned it without showing any emotion on her rigid countenance. I rested my arm on the open window door and said, "Hi, Blanche. Sorry to disturb you, but I was hoping to do a story on the Red River Coalition's future."

"Let's have some herbal tea over on the veranda. Park in front of the house, I'll be there shortly," she said, then continued her conversation with the hired hand.

I pulled up to the log cabin castle and sat in the shade of the cantilevered roof. I watched Blanche slowly come my way, and then head south as if to avoid the connection we were about to make.

Twenty minutes later a woman in a white blouse and purple sarong rounded the corner balancing a serving tray with a teapot and cups above her left shoulder. In her right hand were rolled up placemats. "Hi," she announced. "Blanche said you might want tea."

"Hi. Where did you come from? At first I thought you were Blanche."

"Door around back. It's to the main kitchen." She smiled while arranging everything on a side table between a vacant chair and me. Then she poured a cup and watched as I sipped the brew. "I'm Theresa, part time office assistant, other times servant to this institution. Just holler if you need anything else." And off she went in the direction Blanche Banyan had just appeared from. They looked a lot alike.

"How do you like the tea? The herbs are grown right here on the ranch," said Blanche. Or was it Theresa, I wondered.

"Great, but I have to admit I wasn't expecting such hospitality," I said, though it was extremely bitter, even with two spoons of sugar. "What's it called?"

"Nodus Respite," she said. I must have looked puzzled or dazed because she quickly added, "meaning a relief from the complexities of life, even though it's loaded with caffeine."

159

"It has a nice ring to it," I said with cup in hand, but it tasted so awful I had to put it down.

"What brings you out this way instead of phoning?" Suddenly, she seemed anxious and tense, or irritated at my reposed state. "I thought we had concluded everything during our last interview."

"You weren't at the public hearing for the Sorrow Creek environmental impact study the commissioners held last week," I said, trying not to piss her off more than she already was. "It's a story I'm working on and was wondering what the opposition is to the Sorrow Creek project. The coalition's response, that is."

"It wasn't that big a deal. And if you were there you'd know it already. What you are doing is grasping at straws—still trying to sensationalize everything…"

"It's my job, all right? You won't answer your phone or return calls, and you don't bother showing up."

"I had more important things going on that I don't need to explain to you. Especially you."

"I understand, but just for the record, why not at least give me a short quote."

"Because the topic was about a preliminary outline," she said. "What needs to be addressed is part of the public forum, and *that* I've actually contributed to already. Something you should be well aware of by now. Or something you can look up for the record. And besides, I've told you I'd let you know when's the appropriate time to respond," she snapped back. "And now's not the time. Topping the list of priorities is reestablishing a foothold that was left behind with the passing of Derrick. There's your quote."

"Okay, but I've got a deadline, and so far it's a lopsided story."

"I won't be pressured from you or any other newspaper. There will be a statement issued after our board meeting. Until then you can say we're in the process of reorganization," she said bluntly.

I sat back in the Adirondack chair and tried another sip of tea, then quoted Henry Adams about meaning: "No one means all he says and yet very few say all they mean, for words are slippery and thought is viscous." She looked at me in disbelief. "I just thought it was appropriate is all."

"And I suppose you think it's funny," she said flatly. "You're pushing the envelope while being a complete asshole, you know?"

"That's not what I came out here for. I wanted it to be amicable. That's all."

"You've overstayed your welcome."

"I know that, and I'm sorry you feel that way. I thought of your husband as a true fighter for righteous causes. A really decent guy, the way he was always looking out for the environment instead of dollar signs. At the memorial service, you told everyone Derrick's mission to save the planet would live on even after his death."

"Things have changed," she said and left it at that.

After leaving Banyan's place, I dialed Jen from the Kum & Go convenience store not far from town. Having lost my cell phone, the replacement black pay phone I used was so grimy and scarred with multiple wounds in the dull chrome surface it looked like it was about to be disconnected from life. Even with a little mouth to receiver resuscitation, an utterance could barely be heard on the other end.

"Wily, where are you?" crackled Jen's voice from the fractured earpiece.

"At the Kum & Go." I described to her what I'd been doing.

"So what do we have here, Casanova?"

"Very little since Blanche wasn't taking the stand, I mean a stand on anything."

A long pause ensued before she stuck me with the same blunt statement I'd heard more than a few times in my life. "I hope you're coming in soon. I need to see your stuff now."

"Shit. Where did the time go?" I was less than happy about a tight noose around my remaining minutes before deadline. "I haven't eaten anything and there's a touch of nausea in the air."

"You should have plenty of time, knowing you're proclivity for work."

"That *really* makes me feel better. It's hardly enough time to breathe. I'm beginning to feel short of breath even as we speak."

"And to think I was hoping to make you happy." She giggled into the receiver. "Now hurry home, darling, I miss those mysterious big brown eyes of yours staring at the computer screen."

Jen's demands put me in convenience store mode. I quickly grabbed a Styrofoam container of stale coffee and headed toward the office. I needed to get cranked up for deadline.

Then it felt like the flu had flown into my stomach. The queasy feeling came with the

162

lukewarm coffee reduced to a thick black concoction so acidic that it ate at my stomach lining. That, and riding around in a car without AC when it was one hundred and five outside.

Along with an increasing amount of sweat, I had become delusional in that drugged out sort of way, feeling paranoid about possibly being poisoned.

I drove down Progress Avenue. On the right was a laundromat, the old movie theater, a hardware store and sporting goods shop. To the left was a bank, the small grocery store, and along the next block, an old red brick housing unit converted into an insurance agent office, a CPA firm, a dress shop and a chiropractor. Everything one could ask for in life existed somewhere on main street. I stopped at a drug store to get some antacid, but the place looked to be closed.

Time runs short in an adrenaline-induced state of working under deadline. Arriving at the office a little on edge seemed to help me avoid distraction. Engrossed with a deadline of her own, Jen seemed neither happy nor relieved to see me. She didn't care; it was a race to the finish for both of us.

I went through the ritual of cranking out copy without speaking to anyone except Tuck, who was unaware of the high-pressure system building in my brain.

"So what's tomorrow's news?" Tucker muttered behind his computer wall without looking over the top of the screen.

"How's this sound? Sorrow Creek becomes a reality over Banyan's dead body."

He kept typing without missing a beat, then saying, "Did you have to gaze into your crystal ball for that scoop?"

"Seeing if you were listening. What's up on the gambling scene?"

Tucker continued typing at a frenzied pace. "Haven't you heard? There's renewed interest in real estate and commerce. Boom times, buddy. Boom times are here again. Some think the gambling craze could actually happen."

"You gotta believe in something." In my peculiar state it was delusions of reality. Everything seemed distorted to some degree, and sometimes even physically, listing to one side or the other while trying to maintain balance.

"Even if you don't," said Tucker. "Ain't nobody in his right mind wants to see his hometown get'n trashed with the likes of gambling and whoring," he deadpanned his hick impersonation. "But they'll sell their soul to the devil for the right price."

"Rusty must be hyperventilating over the possibilities. But is it true that there really is a whore under every bush when gambling comes to town?" I had lost control of the conversation; however Tucker pulled it back into perspective.

"What's it matter as long as there's hope." He didn't wisecrack or miss a keystroke when answering.

"What sluts we are. A country full of starving reporters that'll write anything for the little crumbs life feeds us. I got your headline for tomorrow's edition: *Reporter Flatlines on Deadline*. And the way I feel, it could be an omen of things to come."

"Does your attitude need some attention, Spiver?"

"Just looking for a little sympathy from the devil, is all."

Tucker's frantic keyboard clacking finally came to a halt. He paused to insert in the conversation: "You picked the right place but it sounds like you're doing a pretty good job of it on your own, buddy."

I needed to put something in my stomach, but it was a billboard in Vegas that fed my hallucination. What came to mind was this grease spot serving breakfast and lunch. The diner's slogan read: "*We keep Fry'n Til the Sun Quits Shine'n*", and below it was a picture of a leggy vivacious waitress in a short black and white outfit that almost gave a pubic viewing. Her dazzling eyes were directed toward the heavens, one leg was bent at the knee, and she rested a platter of crispy chicken on her shoulder in front of three smiling cooks in sparkling white cylindrical chefs' hats.

Although I was in the midst of a billboard fantasy, there was a strong desire to have Blanche Banyan fried for disorienting my mind from drinking her herbal tea concoction.

Luckily, in my reporter's notebook I had scribbled a pile of unused notes and quotes on Derrick Banyan and the Sorrow Creek project. In some wild way he lived on in the old files for the next day's edition. The lead-in went:

Sorrow Creek Opposition Ebbs
At Commissioners' Hearings

Like the receding water lines of Lakes Powell and Mead, opposition to the Sorrow Creek project has also begun to evaporate.

The alarming rate of evaporation for most southwest water projects was one of many concerns opponents had toward the proposed Sorrow Creek reservoir 10 miles west of Great Valley.

Leading the charge against the project was the late Derrick Banyan and his Red River Coalition. However, any movement by the coalition to preserve Sorrow Creek Basin and watershed from a large-scale development has failed to materialize at several public hearings to determine the project's environmental impact.

According to Blanche Banyan, acting chairperson, the coalition is currently undergoing reorganization after Banyan's death. Banyan declined to say what the coalition's future plans are and whether or not they will continue to fight the proposal.

During this past public hearing before the commissioners, there had been a noticeable absence of any registered coalition member opposing NRI's intention to create a reservoir in the basin and a luxury retirement community surrounding it.

The late environmentalist, Derrick Banyan, had vehemently opposed the project up until his death from a car accident outside his ranch. His objections to the project created resentment and animosity among the community leaders, even though he claimed the project would deplete the region's valuable water resources and do irreparable harm to a sensitive ecosystem and wildlife habitat.

Jeannette didn't say anything while editing the story until she finished. "You're telling me no one said anything negative about the project at an environmental hearing?"

"That's not what was in the story. I simply stated the coalition had lost steam in opposing it. I could tell there were a few people that didn't like the proposal, but the meeting's format was more informative than confrontational. Nobody spoke out against any particular issue. They mostly asked questions, I guess saving up for a debate later on. If you want I'll add more, but I doubt it would add anything to the story."

"That's your opinion. But no, it's fine like it is. You did good making it the right length for the hole I need to plug." She rolled her eyes and laughed. "Lighten up, you look like a ghost, you're face's so pale. Are you sick or something?"

A squeamish feeling was working its way through my system. Being under the threat of deadlines was a hell of a way to live. But it all came down to shit or get off the pot. Or just flush down the rest of the crap that surfaced from nausea. At first, when the stomach ache hit, I thought it was due to a lethal batch of tea and coffee, but the queasiness persisted until I ran to the restroom and bowed before the throne. It wasn't until hurling what was left of my innards into a swirling eddy, that I felt clear again.

Almost everyone had left by the time I pulled myself together enough to emerge from the bowels of the restroom and see Jeannette still at her desk. Surprisingly, she had waited. I walked back to the editorial department and sat at my own desk, eyes closed to the abysmal recovery process of feeling human again.

"You did a fantastic job putting those stories together, considering your fragile condition," she said from her desk, between little gasps of air as if trying to restrain an uncontrollable laugh.

"You have a bizarre sense of humor," I muttered helplessly in my dark despair.

"Relax. It could have been worse. You could have gotten sick before deadline."

"Well, if that isn't a relief. But it felt like an axe splitting my guts all the same."

"Ouch! Guessing you must be feeling pretty miserable."

"I thought you loved me," I whimpered.

"I do, Wily," she mockingly whimpered in return.

"If it wasn't for you, I would have quit Rusty long ago. You know that?"

"I love your persistence. You're such a sweetheart, but don't let me hold you back from attaining your true goals in life."

"I couldn't ask for anything more than being with you."

"All right, cut the crap. It's not some attempt at getting laid, is it?"

"I'm in need of something to settle my stomach. How about some fried chicken?"

"Some other time. The hubby seems pissed all of a sudden now that I'm leaving. I don't want to compound the issue with a public showing."

"It's not like we're going to some strange motel."

She stood up from her desk, smiled, and said that was exactly the plan.

To avoid suspicion we left at separate times. I went first and Jen followed shortly after. Hunger had become a real issue, and I hoped there was something to eat back at the room, like smoked oysters instead of a can of worms.

I felt guilty about not seeing Lucy for the second time we were supposed to connect. But then again, she had probably hooked up with that biker and was traveling around the country with him.

14

Surprisingly, I awoke early. The sky was clear and bright for the moment, but it hadn't always been that way. I grew up in Vegas when they were testing a lot of atom bombs.

A popular family pastime when a bomb was about to explode was to hit Wimpy's drive-in on Fremont Street. With Servus Fone in hand, we'd order atomburgers, fries and shakes and head out to the test site in my mother's 1958 Oldsmobile. We would picnic with hundreds of others at a secluded desert spot northwest of town near Frenchman Flat. To top off the occasion, Mother sported her rendition of the Atomic Hairdo, almost like the original, designed by a hairdresser at the Flamingo. But the Old Man insisted it was more of a blonde busby than a mushroom.

Then, with all of the other gawkers, we waited for the flash on the horizon; terror and awe coexisting in the same frame. There was a sun exploding with its fiery center spreading across the horizon. Afterwards, the immensity of the sky condensed into gray matter, which produced ground tremors and a sticky dust storm. And oohs and aahs from satisfied viewers.

After gazing at the day for a moment, I took a cool shower, as if to wash away a residue of delirium from being drugged by Blanche Banyan. My guess was witches' brew in the teapot, causing an erratic reaction to my lovemaking hours later, not sure if Jen liked it, loved it or simply took it in stride. It was more an anticlimax than orgasmic, even with a couple of scotches between us.

It had been harder for me to get into the spirit of things with all of the commotion in my life those last couple of days. Too tired to do anything else, I went back to bed and dozed off to a dream with a window seat and view of a firing range the length of Death Valley. Looking down I saw Lucy with a shotgun aimed directly at me like I was a piece of skeet. Terror set in like the kind a sticky dust storm produces. And there was guilt staring back at me. Because Lucy had all those feature attractions, including a wicked sense of reality that I failed to take advantage of when given the chance.

In what seemed like only a few minutes, I was awakened by the customary pounding of headboards hitting the wall next to mine. It happened at least three times a night depending on the new neighbors' enthusiasm. But from outside the gray matter of my brain, someone was at the door instead of the bed.

"Wily! You in there?" called a vaguely recognizable female voice. Maybe only my name sounded familiar, I wasn't sure at first.

"Who is it?" I crackled, sounding strange even to myself.

"What do you mean, who is it? It's Jeannette. I'm heading to work but need to talk to you about the Blanche story."

"I'll be right there," I yelled through the door. She always got what she was after from me. And I looked forward to seeing her and thinking about what might transpire again. However, last night's fray dampened any sort of urgency.

Anyhow, her steadfast loyalty to the *Great Valley Beacon* and Rusty Gates kept it at a professional level in the mornings. I was hoping that would change with the number of times she might stop by. But I didn't press her since she was still unhappily married. With limited enthusiasm, I draped a flannel shirt over the old gray tee shirt and boxer shorts and unhooked the chain.

"Um," she intoned pleasantly, compared to the chaos of the previous night.

She continued to stand in the doorway. "Just thought I'd see if you were going to be on time. Rusty called early this morning. He'd read the masterpiece on Banyan's coalition and wanted to see you before it went to press." I was touched by the mockery while wishing there was more to her stopping by than flashing a warning signal.

"I'll be at the office in fifteen, just have to shave," I promised, hoping it wasn't a lie.

"Rusty'll be pissed if you miss him before deadline."

"Isn't *that* a forgone conclusion?"

After shaving, I rushed out into the unknown, arriving at the office shortly before ten. Meanwhile, things had become twisted. Rusty sat at Jeannette's desk, eyes on the computer screen. Jen, standing behind him, turned and smiled when I walked past them. Then I thought worse of the situation. It was depressing to think Rusty was to the point of wanting to completely manipulate the press.

"Good morning," I cheerfully said, but it sounded all wrong, gruff and lacking sincerity.

"It's all relevant." Rusty said without looking up from the screen. He lit a cigarette and went back to reading. "What in the hell is up with this piece you wrote yesterday?"

My heart skipped a few beats. "Just another angle in the scheme of things."

"How 'bout we drop all the fun and games."

Jen shot me a puzzled look with raised shoulders. "Anything wrong, Rusty?" she asked.

"Just about everything," he sighed aloud and added, "Damn it, Spiver, let's get the fucking story straight and quit the crap about stirring up opposition to Sorrow Creek and the gaming issue. Damn it, I want this all to work in our favor, as does the rest of the community. It's a financial fucking gold mine."

"You got it, Hoss." I said.

"Good. At least we got that straight."

Jen walked me to my desk and apologized for Rusty's attitude. I was feeling that my journalistic career was about to take another step backward, similar to previous relationships with women and work.

"It couldn't have been helped though." She tried to explain in simple terms that it was Saville who compromised everything.

173

What a shame, I thought. Another missed opportunity to play with fate. After working for enough papers, reporting had become as natural as gambling. They both provided a regular adrenaline rush, a byproduct of the risks and rewards of playing the game.

After work I walked toward my car in the shadows of semi-darkness, which had swiftly spread below the shale bluffs surrounding town. In the distance was the sound of a dribbling basketball, accentuating the feeling of the hot spring night. To cool things off I met Tucker for a beer at the Portal. In the dusky bar with its mix of clientele, Tucker wanted to know if I had heard anything about Rusty's plan to sell the paper to his Laughlin buddies or Victor Saville.

"No," I said. The prospect was startling. "Wow. Is it true?"

"I think it's possible, but nothing's concrete yet," said Tucker.

That vaguely explained Rusty's suspicious nature of avoidance to any controversy. But I was taken aback at the thought Jeannette might have known and hadn't mentioned it to me.

I tried pumping Tucker for more information, but he swore he knew nothing other than Rusty wanting out of the business. "So what you're saying is that you won't divulge your sources?"

"You know if I could . . ."

"Come on, Tuck. It means a lot to me. If I'm kept out of the loop, it might cause emotional damage to my psyche."

"What's that supposed to mean?"

"You know, in Greek mythology where a young woman falls in love with Eros and becomes the personification of the soul."

"So what's that have anything to do with the sale of a newspaper?"

"It's more a matter of trust. I think I'm falling in love with Jen. It'll tear me apart if she knew about Rusty selling out like this and didn't say anything about it." I said in earnest.

But Tucker was rolling his eyes. "What difference does it make how I found out? We don't even know if it's a sure deal. Maybe Saville will be the buyer. Who knows what Rusty's capable of doing?"

"That's why he likes those trips to Nevada." I said, more out of paranoia at losing the job than simple curiosity about Rusty's agenda.

"You know, anything seems possible with a desperate high stakes gambler."

I played along with the idea that rumor could be construed as truth. "Rusty's way of thinking is part of a widespread dementia lingering from the area's boom and bust cycles. What I've noticed while being in Great Valley is everyone who attempts to make it bigger than is possible ends up losing more than they've gained."

"At least it's a predictable trend that keeps everybody temporarily employed," he said and drank his beer.

"Hey," Tuck shouted; I sprung out of my reverie. "You know why Rusty keeps pushing for more positive spin on everything? So he can keep the paper looking legit. He's probably used the paper to leverage his gambling debts."

"So our present job situation is nebulous?" I said, sipping off the foam on my second draw and feeling a little nebulous myself. " . . . And Rusty, the small time publisher under the influence of grandeur and women, is really only a mere pawn in some demented chest game played by his female friends and casino buddies in Laughlin? And we will have to work for *them*, or Saville."

"Something like that." Tucker drained his glass and stood up from the barstool to leave. Then added, as if reading my emotional query, "Anyway, just between us, I don't think Jen knows anything about it. This sort of thing wouldn't be on the books. It's just what I picked up through the grapevine."

He never revealed his sources. And maybe subconsciously I didn't want to know where the vineyard was, figuring it kept anxiety at an even keel and that everything would unravel in due time. Which it did in more ways than I could shake a pistol at.

15

A week passed in a state of quiet uncertainty, like the Sorrow Creek project, until Victor Saville made an encore performance at the county commissioners' meeting, where everyone continued to review his proposal with great optimism.

Despite my inherent mistrust of Saville and the fact he was *my* main suspect in the death of Banyan, I tried to get along with him during the times we dealt with each other. But Saville wouldn't give me an in depth story about his company's future plans.

While I meandered about in the editorial department of my brain, Rusty plopped down in the seat next to my desk. We faced each other rather pensively, considering the gravity of our situation where mistrust and reality were about to join forces.

"Let's take a walk," was his way of a greeting. Instead of to his office, we strolled to the back room, which was the historical archives department. Clutter competed with space making it the sort of place where one would feel at home in if you were a pack rat. "This will ensure we have some privacy without interruption." He rested half his ass on the long folding table that was used to bind each issue of the *Beacon* and to clip out articles for the 'library' system that looked easily combustible.

"Wily, just wanted to let you know I got a pretty good offer for the paper and I'm thinking of selling." Gates filled the room with smoke. He had lit one of his cigarettes and puffed away with nervous energy. "Not that I really want to . . ." He took in another puff, "but might not have any choice." A long ash fell onto the linoleum floor, making me nervous as well.

"To whom?" I said without alarm. It might be a pleasant change after dealing with Gates.

"A couple of business partners from Laughlin."

"When?"

"Probably close, within the month," Rusty said without any hint of enthusiasm.

But I had to ask anyway: "What about the staff?"

"Some stay, some go. Depends," Gates said.

In order to release tension I looked around for a place to pace among the walls lined with bookcases stacked with old AP stylebooks and bound newspapers. I finally settled back down in the rickety chair, where everything seemed for a moment unbearable, and asked: "What about me?"

Rusty looked up from the ashtray he stubbed his butt in and smiled. "Don't know. Not my decision. But I'll put in a good word. Although you have pissed me off at times, your copy has been first rate. You, Tuck and Jen have made this paper a little profit."

When it came down to the bottom line everything sucked about him selling out, but I wasn't verbally expressing my outrage for his disloyalty. Under the surface it was more about Jeannette than the job. I had been through the axe routine before, only without as much emotional attachment.

"What about the stories?"

"Just keep 'em coming, like nothing's changed. It's still up in the air until the offer is firm and the money's in the bank. Actually I'd like to dress up the paper so it's worth more."

He was sitting on the edge of the table, lighting another cigarette. It was hard to judge if it was good or bad news for Rusty Gates. He was in a contemplative mood where conversation was always on the edge of some indefinite direction. He did manage to indicate that there were a few parties involved in the transaction, including someone from the charter service.

"So," I said, "When did this happen?" Everything was suspiciously unclear.

"Been talking to these guys for a while, but they made a solid offer if the gambling initiative goes through."

"Fat chance, don't you think?"

"I sort of figure about fifty-fifty," he said confidently.

"So depending on the gaming vote, I'd still have a chance of keeping my job?"

"Let's just hope it passes. I don't want to see anyone disappointed if it fails." Rusty was avoiding any potential for deceiving me or giving the pretense I still had a future there.

I told Gates about my visit from Victor Saville and the story he found on the laptop, which probably had by now suffered a horrible death. He didn't care, only saying I shouldn't write things I didn't want others to read.

"So, what are you going to do about it? Call the cops?"

"Yeah, that would help the situation," I responded sarcastically. "I thought you two were buddies, so you might want to quiet him down."

"Don't worry about it. I'll buy you a new laptop. How's that sound?"

"It's not about the fucking computer. It's not even about being violated. Something's happening here that really sucks."

"Yeah, well, don't go making it worse by complaining about something you're not prepared to do anything about."

It was sound advice and something I already knew from my days working for Rudy Morris. Eventually everyone was dealt a bad hand, said Morris when confronted with occasional scrapes. The studio lights never dimmed on Morris' porno empire despite his adversaries.

Once an advertisement for *Vegas Vanity* had been plastered on a street barricade. Days later the entire barricade was destroyed, including orange reflectors—smashed into bits of plastic shards—and the picture of a slinky woman on the poster defaced beyond recognition. The only thing Rudy Morris ever said about the incident: "There's always some dumb motherfucker out there making it rough on everyone, including the street sweeper."

180

After leaving Rusty's office, I walked over to Jeannette's desk. I stuck my head directly above her. Her long brown hair hung in a ponytail down the back of her beige blouse where the outline of her bra showed through. She had cocked her head sideways, glancing upward, smiled at first, then frowned. My first guess was she felt sorry for me, but realized I was wrong when she started to laugh.

"A real scream," I said, ruffled at her audaciousness. She calmly told me to relax and then agreed to have lunch. Although Jeannette had a questionable sense of humor the thought of eating together cheered me up.

On the edge of town was Wild Bill's Steak House. It was rustic and western with the bar and dining room blending together like scotch and soda. The walls were paneled with amber knotty pine, the tables rough-hewn planks draped with red and white checkered tablecloths, and everyone sat on benches made from split logs that had repeatedly gouged the hardwood floor. The place drew in a cross section of people: roadies, rowdies, truck drivers and families crisscrossing the American landscape, looking for some respite from the heat.

Jen ordered a coke and sandwich, but spent more time chewing on the straw than drinking. I went on about the paper changing hands and the prospect of losing my job. She'd roll her dreamy blue eyes around when I repeatedly mentioned the coincidence of Rusty getting the offer right after Saville stole the laptop.

Jen didn't seem to care. Eventually her roving eyes focused on a family with kids seated next to us;

181

tourists, quibbling about what to order. She smiled at them and openly admired the couple's two little girls. Everything *seemed* to glide effortlessly along. The waitress was jovial and frequently filled my coffee cup. She knew Jen and made small talk when she finally showed up with my order. I smiled, but didn't hear what was said between them as my plate with a half-pound cheeseburger and fries caught my attention.

I was generously applying mustard and ketchup when I glanced up and noticed the lunch crowd had begun to thin, opening up a clear shot into the bar area where Victor Saville and Rusty Gates grabbed a seat. They ordered cocktails, while I bit into the burger and looked down at the plate to avoid eye contact. The plate took on the appearance of a painter's pallet of a red and yellow mix that had oozed from between the bun. When I looked up again, Jeannette and the waitress were still engaged in conversation, talking as if it was a shocking revelation that some mutual friend with three kids had a husband who'd slept with the neighbor's wife.

After about fifteen minutes, Gates and Saville stood to leave. Rusty pulled his cowboy hat over his head and reached for his wallet, paying the bill. I choked a little on the dry bun, which drew Jen's attention.

The waitress went off to collect the tab from another table in the bar. I sopped up the last pile of ketchup with a cold fry and asked Jen about Victor Saville's connection with the sale of the paper. She just shrugged and picked at her food.

For the first time since we met, I was feeling disconnected. Our relationship diminished by many degrees from the heat of passion to an aloof coolness. It might have been caused by the detachment in her tone throughout lunch; it might have been mine. I wasn't sure which, since we had hardly talked. Blame it on the waitress or my inquisitive nature as to what Saville and Gates were planning. The bottom line was, we had been preoccupied with other things throughout the meal.

Finally, I leaned forward, breaking our silence with: "Why do I have this crazy feeling that I'm being left in the dark?"

"I don't know what you mean," she said, eyes caught in a double cross. Maybe guilty of deception? "Rusty didn't fill me in on the details, if that's what you're implying."

"Give me a break." Irritation forced a rise in my voice. I was incensed at being kept out of the loop, and it was starting to show.

"What the hell am I supposed to say? Rusty swore me to secrecy."

"You're supposed to tell me everything. I thought we were in love and should be able to confide in each other. Right?" I had stepped over the bounds: This was an affair not a relationship. So inwardly I laughed and cried at the defeat. "— Okay, I know it sounds like a crock . . ."

"There's a chance Saville might be part owner of the *Beacon*. . . or his company. I'm not sure which."

I uttered a piercing "Ouch" from the pain and fear of thinking the axe might literally be the axe. "Shit. Who would be the other partners?"

"Evan Shade, the charter service guy. Don't know any of the rest."

"Those are our future bosses?" My jaw started to hang lower until it dropped onto both knuckles. "What the . . ."

"I might look for another job," she said, and looked down at her untouched chicken-salad sandwich with chips, then at my head propped up by elbows resting on the checkered table.

"Leaving me?"

"I didn't say that. But if you think Rusty ran a fucked-up operation wait until you see what these guys are capable of doing."

16

The breakdown happened after covering a feature story down valley. The once fluid motion of the car had evaporated after overheating. I pulled onto the shoulder as steam temporarily blurred my vision. The coolant had dried on the windshield to a thick coat of greenish slime under a blistering sun. Temperatures had already reached ninety, but under the hood it felt like a hundred and ninety as I worked desperately at the radiator cap trying to relieve pressure. It took a rag saturated with the scalding stickiness to realize a broken radiator hose had left me stranded.

I stood smoldering beside the car, letting my thumb do the talking as I tried hitchhiking back to town. I'd been on my way back to the office after wrapping up a feature interview with an exchange student from India who was staying with a ranch family. The typical fluff piece would run on the new 'educational page'. Rusty thought the *Beacon* needed to reinforce the paper's commitment to education.

So what had I done to deserve where I was? Karma was one thing. In reality nothing was a sure thing, no afterlife-time guarantees or money-back policies at the store of unfulfillment. The Swiss author, Max Frisch, had it right when he wrote: "It's precisely the disappointing stories, which have no proper ending and therefore no proper meaning that sound true to life."

And I believed it. Especially when an old, rusted-out Mustang pulled over. I recognized it with surprise. Lucy was at the wheel. It had been about two weeks since I last saw her, passed out. She wore a black muscle shirt and blue jeans. She had a dark tan. Her black hair was pinned to the back of her head, but also spiked in all directions from driving with the windows down. I got in beside her.

Although Lucy looked a little frayed around the edges, she was an immense visual experience, like a mirage come true. Not only did she appear so ravishing, but I had thought seeing her again would be a long shot at best.

"Wow, look what the Mustang dragged home," I said, and got in beside her, sticking to the vinyl seat from a drenching sweat storm I had conjured up from hours of pacing. "The last time we were together you were locked in the grip of the sandman, and then later everybody thought you had been kidnapped or something."

"Really?" she shrieked to the roadside attraction she had acquired on her way into town. "I can't believe they think he kidnapped me."

"Not really. They thought you and he robbed the cash box and made a quick getaway," I said, observing her expression of mild irritation behind a

186

pair of classic, big black-rimmed, '50s style, Ray Ban sunglasses. We sat motionless for awhile, listening to what sounded like a hummingbird, a cricket or the piercing squeal of a fan belt or water pump bearings. She seemed oblivious to the noise, or more likely just didn't care.

"The asshole stole the money and took off after I fell asleep. Like I was date-raped or something, but I don't think he touched me. I couldn't face Eloy, so I decided it was a good time to follow my dreams, or nightmares, whichever came first," she said from one side of her mouth. The other side held a Marlboro that was inserted into the car's cigarette lighter she was holding. She inhaled vigorously for a puff and reinserted the lighter.

"Which was . . .?"

"Vegas," she puffed.

"Have a good time?"

"It was all right. But when I tried finding a singing job on my own, they told me I'd have to strip as part of the act. What a hole. Except I snagged a small bit in a lounge act, finally."

"Where at?"

"Sid's City."

"Wow, the big time. Congratulations on kicking butt instead of showing it at the burlesque. But isn't that part of Victor Saville's conglomerate?"

"I thought, what the hell, I'd drop his name and see what'd happen. It sucks, I know. I thought it was below my standards. But I was getting desperate. Come to find out, Vegas is hard on chicks. So I used him as a reference and they let me audition. They were in rehearsals anyway."

"So you didn't have to see him?"

187

She gave me that sidelong glance and smiled. "I didn't say that. No. We had a couple of drinks when he met me in the lounge after my act."

"I bet it was frustrating having to drink with that creep. But I know; you needed a job. Sometimes it can't be helped when you have to search your purse instead of the soul for tangible answers to life's universal questions."

"Wily, you're crazy. I know you're pissed at the guy. I'm guessing because Victor has made me happy for the first time in a long time and you're jealous of my good luck. Right?"

"Okay, I admit it. But Saville might have had something to do with Banyan's death. And it's a pretty strong conviction on my part."

"I've got to tell you. Victor is sort of a friend. Always has been since he checked in at the motel. That's one of the reasons he likes to stay there. And it's not that he's screwing me either. Like someone I know," she said, staring intently into my eyes. "I'm not his type, anyway. Besides, if he wants to get laid there are enough women in his harem. He could take them along wherever he goes."

"Lucy, he's a fucking gangster."

"So what. Half the politicos in Great Valley could be considered gangsters, the way they operate. Look at your boss, Rusty Gates. Anyway, Victor's been nice to me. And, for now, he got me my dream job."

"Congratulations. I wouldn't have believed it."

"Yeah, right. Wily, you're lucky too. You know Saville was just about ready to come after you for constantly fucking with him. And he would of but didn't want to mess with some family ties. You know he had nothing to do with Banyan's accident. He didn't give a shit about Derrick and that coalition, not enough to ruin their lives anyhow. But he does think you're on to something, like someone wanted to get rid of Banyan."

"I can't believe *he'd* be giving me credit for anything," I said, a little shell shocked. "Does he know who killed Banyan?"

"He doesn't care what happens in this town unless it has to do with the prospect of gambling and water. When I asked about Banyan's death, he said that Derrick was a small inconvenience in the scheme of things, but he guessed the accident worked to his advantage," she said, stubbing her butt out in an already over populated ashtray. She popped the clutch and we lurched forward.

"I guess it's better not to know anything you might not want to know about."

"Tell you what I think?" said Lucy.

"What?"

"Blanche and her sister have something to do with Derrick's crash. Think about it. Banyan was a rich son-of-bitch. Besides being a trust-funder, he was raising shit-loads a cash up until he died. So now what's going to happen to all of it? They gonna give it all to the Red River Coalition — I'm pretty sure I didn't read *that* in the *Great Valley Beacon*."

"No, they said they're in the process of reorganizing or regrouping."

"Blanche and her sister, who I call Ms. DeeCee, are lobbyist shysters. They came on the heels of Derrick; one of those do-gooders they could see coming two-thousand miles away. You should've been doing a little more research instead of hanging out with Jeannette all the time."

We began rolling at a high rate of speed with the windows down, making conversation difficult. So I let it go and we stopped talking for a while. The hot desert wind was refreshing at first, but distressing later as the air became stifling and the wind unsettling.

Life on a hard drive. What was a person to do? Damned if you did and damned if you didn't. So I compromised, and put the window up halfway in order to concentrate as to why she never wanted to tell me who drove the red Blazer.

"You know something that's been nagging me ever since you left here? Not that I care anymore."

She said, surprised, "What are you talking about?"

"The owner of the red Blazer who was staying at the Lucky U."

"We never had a chance after I fell asleep in the lobby. And I had to get out of there since Munn thought I stole his money."

"I don't think your step-dad is pressing charges, but he probably *did* think you took the money," I yelled above the howling sound of the wind, breaking what little concentration I had left.

"I don't care about that. He can get screwed. Besides, it's about time he gave a little at the office. Eloy's got more money than Vegas has whores," she said after rolling her window half way up so we could talk.

I wasn't sure how many whores that could have been exactly, but didn't doubt Eloy had enough

190

money to buy every hooker in town a few times over. Then I asked her if she was going back to her old job. She seemed a little hyper, like someone who might have taken a case of no-doze as an appetizer.

"No way in hell. I just came back to square with Eloy and get my shit. Can't wait to move to Vegas," she said while trying to light another Marlboro with the radio knob she had inadvertently pulled off thinking it was the lighter.

"Think you can slow down and relax a little."

"I've been driving for the past 12 hours on nothing but coffee and cigarettes and it's wearing me a little thin."

We were getting close to Banyan's place when Lucy blurted out she and Banyan had had a thing going for awhile, but it ended when his Washington girl friend found out about it. "Ms. DeeCee threatened me. Told me to stay away from Derrick or there'd be dire consequences. I could've cared less about him, I told her. Anyway, it wasn't anything more than a one night stand."

"I thought we were talking about Saville. What made you want to bring all of this up about Banyan?" I had pretty much lost interest in pursuing any additional angles of the Banyan saga. Even my mental notes, what little I had left, were diminishing since hearing the paper was going to be sold.

"We're coming up on Banyan's exit," she yelled above the din of the wind, as if I were deaf. "And besides, Blanche's sister is the one with the red Blazer. There, you happy now?"

"You mean that flighty gal pretending to be Blanche's assistant and kitchen help? I thought she looked vaguely familiar."

"I don't know about all that, but, yeah. That's the one. Ms. DeeCee hooked up with Derrick about a year and a half ago. There was this long-distance dating thing going on between the two, about the same time I met Derrick. We went out together a couple of times." She looked over at me to see my reaction.

"I'm stunned. How come you never told me before?"

"It never came up and when it did you were always too busy working, asshole. Remember those times? Anyway, shortly after Ms. DeeCee starts hanging around, Blanche makes the scene and steals the show. Then marries the bastard a couple of months later. I think the two sisters were always conniving together, but Blanche was the ringleader."

"You mean nobody knew they were sisters?"

"They had different names, who would know unless someone did some research, Wily."

"You giving me a hard time?"

"Sure, as much as I can." Her smile was intoxicating and I hadn't had anything to drink.

As we approached the exit at seventy-five miles an hour, my hand pointed right against the glass. "Mind taking it?" The question came out in a whisper, as if being sucked or forced out by ill logic. I wished it had never left my mouth: We were going way too fast to negotiate a safe exit and I probably would've felt a little more than guilt for causing a wreck.

But Lucy went into a high-speed swerve off the highway and onto the exit ramp, which sloped downward to the old frontage road and a four-way stop. On the right, next to the road, the Red River ran the rapids in whitecap frenzy like Lucy's driving.

"Thanks for getting off," I wheezed through weakened lung capacity from the G-force pinning my shoulder against the door.

"For those special moments in life when you feel like taking chances." She flashed me a lunatic look. "Hold on." She headed down the road paralleling the river. Before we approached Banyan's sprawling spread, there was a sign saying 'Great Valley Town Limits' and below in smaller letters: 'Pop. 12,950'

Lucy shrieked after reading that. "Man, that's a fucking lie. It hasn't been that since people found out about oil shale." Then she wanted to know where Banyan had gone off the road.

"Soon after we pass the entrance to Banyan's place: At mile marker 113." I breathed with relief when she began decelerating and eventually came to a stop at the spot.

We stared at rocks and a serious lack of moisture along an embankment where dried-out weeds resembled neglected hash browns on a blackened grill of asphalt rubble. At the bottom of a ravine was a canopy of cottonwood trees and the shady banks of a river loaded with carp, whitefish and the nearly extinct razorback chub. It wasn't exactly the place to take a fishing trip, but it didn't stop us from catching a glimpse of the accident scene.

There wasn't much to see accident-wise at mile marker 113 with Mother Nature's wondrous ways at housekeeping, and the help of a tow truck. It didn't look like anything had occurred, much less a catastrophe. Wagon trains, Indians and other things with horsepower had cruised this area for centuries and yet the only signs of civilized destruction were the road we stood beside and the indigenous high-tension power lines strung between towers. Like something the Man de la Mancha would also see as a formidable enemy. Or Derrick Banyan.

"This is where it all took place," I said, surveying the landscape with little enthusiasm. We were about three miles past the entrance to Banyan's ranch. I didn't know where the property boundary was, but it wasn't inconceivable that he and the razorback chub once owned the entire stretch of river we stood along.

"Let's walk around there. See if we find anything," said Lucy, starting down the embankment, sliding on scree in her cowboy boots then galloping out at the bottom.

"The cops have gone through here with a fine-tooth comb. And I got to get back to the office. You done?" I yelled from above.

"No," she hollered firmly.

I formed a megaphone by cupping hands around my mouth and shouted back, "Is this some attempt to get me in the weeds."

"Don't flatter yourself. Either get down here or start hitching again. Take your pick, because I can't keep yelling up at you."

I joined her at the bottom and we walked around looking for anything in particular—maybe a car part, some souvenir or keepsake Lucy wanted to remember Banyan by. I didn't know. By appearances, Lucy was intent on finding something. She stared at the ground, head darting back and forth as she looked through brambly undergrowth of oak brush and sage.

"Hey, look at this, Spiver," she said and kneeled down. In the weeds were two snakes entwined on a winged staff. Sun glinted off the caduceus emblem Lucy had picked up and rubbed clean with her fingers.

"What d'ya suppose this is doing here?" she asked anxiously.

"Some doc making house calls?"

She held it pinched between her thumb and forefinger and shoved it into my face. "Seriously, take a look. This is a sign something's weird, don't you think?"

"Probably some paramedic lost it helping Banyan off the ground," I said, after searching for words that wouldn't sound too graphic or pathetic. It had probably been a pretty ugly scene, like most car wrecks that wreak havoc on the occupants.

Details were sketchy from what the cops had described in their reports. It appeared Banyan had fallen asleep, the vehicle had veered down the embankment, and he had suffered from a head fracture which resulted in a flight from life.

If there was karma, I hoped Derrick Banyan would be traveling in first class since he had championed all of those noble environmental issues by hoping to lower the cancer rate and make the planet a better place to live.

Lucy began looking at the ground again, widening the search perimeter. She moved swiftly through the oak brush, arms flailing with machete-like action to clear a path. She hunched over, thrashed some more at the short stocky branches

195

obstructing her view of the ground, and reached for another object of her attention.

"Here, Wily, check this out," she shouted impatiently.

I headed in her direction, stumbling first on a vine root and becoming entangled in a thicket. "This reminds me of searching for unwanted pricks in a thistle patch."

"Quit your whining and get over here."

In her hand was a Smart Phone. In her mirrored sunglasses was the glare of another day, another moment where things seemed like an unfathomable shock to the conscience.

"What are you looking at?" she said suspiciously.

"Just dazed and confused, and a little surprised at all the litter in this pristine setting."

"It looks like somebody's phone." She held it tightly and examined both sides, opened it and pushed a button.

"Does it work?"

She shook her head. "No. I think the battery's dead. Let's see what else we can find."

I looked around, surveying the landscape for more debris only to have gnats and mosquitoes obscure my concentration. There were other indigenous signs of life among the shale bluffs, brush and asphalt that primarily inhabited the north side of the valley. In the distance was an approaching car.

To be safe we took cover among the trees by the river and watched for any recognizable features of the car. It was shady and slightly cooler as we crouched among the brush and waited for whoever it was to pass.

The reflection off the car's windshield glittered like a Vegas showgirl in a white sequined dress, making it hard to identify the model in the distance.

Red and blue finally bled through the glare, exposing a light bar on top of a cop car. It pulled up behind Lucy's Mustang. Hiding was pointless, so we stood erect and waited. Great Valley's police chief got out of his Crown Vic Police Interceptor, and stared directly at us.

I greeted him by waving hello. He raised his arm high and lashed out a disturbing gesture of command. Then he leaned solemnly against his patrol car, arms folded, until we reached the top of the embankment.

"What were you two doing down there?" he said, pushing away from the car with his butt. The sun was to his back so I still had to squint to get a good look at his expression.

"Looking for my favorite bush, Chief. Didn't know it was private property or would have asked permission."

He ignored me and turned to Lucy. "Your father's been looking for you, young lady."

"I plan on paying him a visit when we're free to leave."

He studied us as if we were a section subparagraph in the violations book.

"I think you ought to plan on paying a little more than that. He didn't press charges but is pretty concerned about the missing money."

"Yeah, well, I didn't take it."

"Who did?" grilled the chief, as he reached for the pen and notepad in his left pocket.

"I don't know his name. He stole it when I fell asleep."

"Who?"

"How should I know?" She paused, swallowed and continued. "One of the hotel guests, a biker-type. If you want a description, then he has long black hair wearing leather. He didn't fill out a registration card with a license number." Lucy hastily added, "Now, if you don't mind, I miss my step-daddy. Can we go?"

"Sure. But, Wily, you'll need to come with me. The people who called in the trespassing report might want to press charges. And if that's the case, Lucy, I'll be in contact later today. You gonna be at the motel?"

"Unless Eloy gives me the boot instead of a mop, which ain't likely to happen."

17

I was feeling a little anxious, but it wasn't the first time I had ridden along with a cop. No matter what town I worked in, whenever things got dull, I'd sign up for the ride-along program and hang with a cop during the night shift. Usually the only action was movements of a high-powered spotlight aimed directly at the thousand or so windows of closed businesses. I hadn't had the luck of personally experiencing the disgusting material police reports are often full of, like domestic violence.

The typical cop beat for the paper was listening to the scanner and hoping for a decent follow-up with some pictures. Most of the time the beat was after-the-fact stories that relied primarily on a censored cop report. Car accidents were, for the most part, straightforward gore. Sometimes the only witnesses were the ones on the front line doing battle, leaving the cops to reconstruct history from tale-tell signs like skid marks, dented guard rails or shredded tread. Fatigue was the only evidence that didn't leave any marks on the road.

I sat sleepily in the patrol car.

"Somebody reported you two trespassing," said the chief. He was looking in my direction when I opened my eyes.

"Who?" I asked. It was a little unsettling to have been picked up on someone's radar screen. They probably saw the Mustang parked along the road and became suspicious or paranoid.

"Blanche Banyan." The chief gave a grin directed at me.

"Don't you think you're getting pretty nit-picky for a guy just wanting to take a piss?"

"You tell me, partner. What were you and the little gal doing down there in the brush?"

"I had a breakdown and Lucy came to my rescue. It's not what it looked like, if that's what you mean."

"Then what was it, Spiver? Snooping around an accident scene?"

"Something like that."

"You find anything you should share with the police? Withholding evidence would be another charge, you know?" He quit smiling and frowned as if startled by his own question of ambiguity.

"If I didn't know any better I'd say you guys covered everything thoroughly."

We continued down the frontage road at 55 miles an hour, half the speed Lucy was probably driving. There wasn't much to look at. Nothing I hadn't gawked at before, like all the sagebrush, dirt and shale cliffs. But I wasn't really much in the mood for sightseeing anyway.

Finally, in the far distance was the jagged, green edge of downtown. Although we were at least five miles from any structure, the town had annexed the surrounding countryside in hopes of a half-million homes being built there during the oil shale boom.

The various trees made it look like an oasis, but under the growth any conception of paradise was belied. On the outskirts of Great Valley were decrepit trailer parks with their aging mobile homes residing next to the decaying rubble of a Union Carbide plant. With its brick and metal skin removed sat the skeletal hulk of an industrial dinosaur.

"My dad worked in that plant," said the chief. "It once processed uranium into yellow cake, a substance used in making atom bombs. The plant not only produced cake, but a number of cancer victims as well." He told me the workers, who had coveted their relatively high-paying jobs, were never told of the dangers from uranium production until well after their shifts had permanently ended. "What a shame. Everybody back then believed it was the best thing that ever came to town."

We drove by a dilapidated radiator repair shop with a swamp cooler on top where swallows had flocked, beaks to the rusted grill, seeking water through the metal slits.

"Those guys will help you out if it turns out to be more than a broken hose," said the chief, pointing to the faded red garage with a yellow sign out front that read, 'Reliable Radiator Service'. "Fixed every broke radiator I ever had, which luckily has only been about five." The chief was adding a little levity to my dilemma, as if we were old pals looking to spend some quality time working on cars together. "They take care of everything under the hood."

"Thanks, I'll remember that. But I think all it is is a hose job."

The chief looked at me dryly, and in a ritual he'd probably performed a thousand times, pulled a cig from his blue uniform, held it in his mouth and lit it with a Bic. He was so smooth that I hardly noticed until smoke clouded the windshield.

"Mind if I smoke?" he asked with a grin. I didn't care. At least he had AC, but what killed me was the window on the passenger side was controlled by the chief, so I could have choked to death.

"It's your life. Funny, uh?" I tried adding my own levity to the air.

"Real good. Care for one?"

"Sure." And with that the entire car filled with smoke until he cracked his and my windows.

"So Wily, do you still think Saville had something to do with Banyan's death. Anything you want to share?"

"I thought you closed the case." I took another puff and nearly gagged from an overdose of smoke.

The chief eyed me as if I had tested negative on a lie detector. "Gates paid me a visit yesterday. He wanted to know if there was any chance the story was true."

So, I thought, Rusty Gates was doing some investigating on his own. "It was sort of a joke. It was a funny little tale. And now everyone is taking it seriously?"

"Sounds like Saville almost had you in stitches," he chuckled in a mocking manner. "No pun intended."

"Funny, uh. Wouldn't that be against the law or something?"

"Depends, if it was self defense . . ."

"That's reassuring. Meaning Saville would get a free pass."

The chief said it was hard to say, "When it's one word against another."

I told him the complete story of having had nothing better to do than fabricate stories when all else had reached a dead end. "Banyan had so many enemies it is amazing some local hadn't mistaken him for a deer and shot him long ago, like in a common hunting accident. What do you think?"

"About what?" asked the chief of police, "Saville murdering Banyan?"

"Or someone. Just how closely did you examine the Jeep he was riding in?"

"Close enough for a crumpled heap." He was visibly pissed at my questioning his authority. "You ought to go back to city council and stay out of the line of fire. There are some people who are very upset with that kind of thinking. Victor Saville being one and myself for another. And if you keep pursuing it without evidence, it could be considered harassment."

"One thing is certain, Saville wouldn't come asking you to press charges."

Now I was convinced somebody had bumped off Banyan. I didn't know who, but it was something in vile form. "That's a good one. Saville is such an upstanding member of the community that it should matter what he thinks?"

"Defamatory or false statements can get a person in a lot of hot water around here. Just a warning, that's all. And unless you have any information otherwise, the Banyan case is closed. If trespassing charges are pressed, which I doubt after our talk, we'll be in contact, Spiver."

The chief nosed the cruiser into a parking spot next to the office. We sat and looked at each other, speechless until I blurted out: "You know, none of what I think about Banyan matters. The paper's going to be sold and it's pretty unlikely I'll be around to write anything much longer."

"Sorry to hear that . . ."

"Not as much as me."

I reached for the door lever and was half surprised to find one that worked.

I was relieved to finally get out of the car. There is something to be said for keeping distances. "See you later," I said and left the chief saying about the same.

It was almost five when I walked through the office door. Jen only glanced up briefly when I stood by her desk, trying to apologize for being late and not calling. I gave her a short version of the situation and quickly explained the dilemma I was in. She studied the computer screen acting more concerned about deadline than if I landed in jail. "Too bad about your car," she finally said when I turned to leave. "What stories haven't you turned in yet for tomorrow's run?"

"Mine, if you'd only listen," I awkwardly joked and strayed off, a little dejected.

"I listened. So what did you and Lucy talk about the whole time?"

"Didn't really have much to say. She went to Vegas to get away from Munn and was going back to get her things when I hitched the ride. We stopped at the crash site, looked around, and when she found

204

the phone the chief showed up. So we really didn't get to discuss anything. I didn't even have a chance to look at the phone. She stuck it in her pocket and drove off. That's the last I saw of her *and* the phone."

The office was quiet, almost tranquil except for the steady hum of fluorescent tubes. Rusty had left. Maybe permanently, I wasn't sure.

There was only the foreign exchange story left to work on. I sat at my desk, taking an hour to compose quotes, notes and to-the-best-of-my-ability recollections of the past four hours. Then I called city hall for a list of the volunteer paramedics for the Greater Valley Fire and Ambulance Protection District. If nothing else I could find out whose cell phone went missing.

I worked until begging Jen for a ride out to my car. Reluctantly she agreed. She stayed at the office while I used her car to pick up some duct tape and a couple of gallons of water, hoping that was all I needed to get to Reliable Radiator.

I drove while she leaned toward me, flirting with her hands. Her left arm wrapped around my shoulder, fingers playing around my ear and hair. Then she moved in for a side lick while putting her right hand in my crotch. Rubbing vigorously on the ole' stick shift, she then unzipped and slid her fingers, then mouth, into the strike zone. She balked, and loosing her grip caused the old bat to go limp.

"What's wrong?" I said while looking down between my lap and the steering wheel.

"So you didn't do Lucy in the weeds?"

"What . . . ?" My right leg quivered and slipped off the gas pedal, producing an erratic speed and an erotic knee-jerk reaction. "That's your interest down there?"

"Just checking your story," she said, while pressing her elbow into my groin and sitting upright, away from me. "Besides, I don't trust your driving."

I stared blankly at the vanishing prospect of getting any further with her, and on the road ahead. Jen leaned back against her door and looked out the windshield. It took about five minutes for her to ask about the upcoming trip to Laughlin. The contest winners had been announced the day before in the *Beacon.* She had told Rusty that it was a bad idea to send me there because of the workload.

"I've got the weekend to get things under control," I said.

"You ought to know that Rusty isn't going to make payroll this time around."

"I know, he told me it's going to be late and he'd make it up to me."

Jeannette laughed. "You're catching on, sweetheart."

18

In Vegas, what sucked afterward was the shrinking wad of cash, mostly from a few rolls of dice on the green felt spread too thinly against the wrong combination of dots, which meant the game was over. I'd lost just about everything.

But *Vegas Vanity* publisher Rudy Morris always offered cash advances. While working for Morris, the only thing that cluttered my mailbox more than bills were credit card applications which I gladly accepted, as many cards as they'd send me, and they were generous. I quit *Vegas Vanity*, leaving town with several Visas and a promise to Morris that I'd pay back everything I owed or return to the magazine as an indentured servant.

However, I felt confident. I had accumulated a healthy line of credit from the cards by shuffling payments and anteing up the minimum. It may not have been as enjoyable as stud poker, but less stressful because of the illusion of always winning with cash in hand.

Both card games had an adrenaline factor. In poker it was felt immediately, with the charge cards it was once a month. The system worked if I was employed most of the time. And even if I wasn't, the corporate cards arrived anyway, personally engraved.

Although I had a lot of credit remaining, the hole was getting deeper. Weeks of motel charges, over a thousand miles in fuel bills, along with restaurants and some of the other necessities of life.

And I had only one paycheck from Rusty. For the first two weeks and it was short. Rusty explaining that he'd make it up to me with the next check, which I never saw. Nor the big raise I was supposed to get to help balance out my checkbook.

I was getting pretty stretched financially and emotionally when everything started coming down at *The Beacon*. I wanted to jump onto Rusty Gates' weekend charter junket to Laughlin while there was still a chance to get out of the debit column. But when I ran it by Jeannette, she laughed with sarcasm, certain that if it wasn't for Gates' crappy, get-rich schemes and promotions, the paper would have made out okay.

"And we wouldn't be in this absolutely shitty situation of worrying about everyone's jobs," she said.

"What, me worry?" The old Alfred E. Newman cliché didn't even get a rise.

"So that's how you want to behave?" she shot back.

And why not, I thought. I worried way too much as it was. We were approaching my car. I'd been

208

driving her Firebird slowly, stalling as much as possible before mentioning the upcoming trip to Laughlin. "You know Rusty Gates wants me to do a cover feature on the Laughlin contest winners flying out this weekend."

"And I can't persuade you otherwise. You're about to be unemployed and you're going to gamble? Get a grip on something besides a one-armed bandit, Wily," she said with mock laughter.

I said, "So why not try and improve my economic status? Since there's not much else going on that weekend . . ."

"What about Lucy finding that cell phone? Why not figure out what's on the damn thing? Who's it belong to? That should make for a weekend chock full of fun."

"I'm working on it. I'm going to get a battery when I'm in Laughlin since there's no place around here that has that brand."

"You know, of course, you can really be a pain in the ass sometimes."

"What's your problem?" I didn't appreciate her attitude, but tried not to show it.

"I just think going off to Laughlin is a pretty shitty thing to be doing right now," she answered, fuming at the notion I might defy her plans.

It wasn't a challenge, but a desire to win back some of what I'd previously lost. "That's because you're not into gambling."

"The whole thing's perverse! That's all."

That's what I loved about Jen. She was just about always right. But at that moment the queen of my heart was in a poker hand in Laughlin. "It's only for two nights."

"Why not make it two weeks, or better yet why come back at all?"

That was harsh and totally unexpected. "What are you talking about?"

"Reality. What keeps you hanging around when you know there's no future here?"

"You and an optimistic view of the present circumstances. And maybe I don't want Banyan's death to remain a complete mystery."

"Wily, I'm worried there won't be anything here for you when you get back. I'm reaching my limit with the whole dilemma. You traipsing off with Rusty to some casino makes everything worse in the long run."

Subconsciously I agreed with her. She had a point. If the paper folded, there wasn't much left for me in Great Valley except her. And even then it was hard to be sure Jen would want to continue our relationship, pending her divorce.

"Going to Laughlin was just an idea," I said abstractedly. I wanted derailment from the direction the conversation was heading. "I haven't made any commitment to Rusty."

However, Gates was desperate to fill the flight quota. It had been a promotion short of its goal. He had committed to filling twelve seats for a two-night stay at the fabulous Moulin Hotel and Casino. It was the $500 buy-in required that left him short. Although the five bills were converted into chips, a person could still get their money back if they didn't play anything. But some of the contest 'winners' had skipped the free trip after realizing the fine print meant putting cash up front.

I initially shrugged it off but the urge to gamble had become overwhelming, to where I couldn't see doing anything else.

"Of course I'd come back to Great Valley. Job or not. I still have you and my Trans Am, you know?" I pointed at the black beast we had just pulled up behind.

"Yeah, broken down on the side of the road. And you'd probably benefit more by leaving me behind as well."

"That's not true," I declared.

"Okay, so you have your car to come back to." Her smile looked like it was painted on. Under the happy face was a frown.

"What about you?"

She said firmly, "Don't be too sure I'll be waiting when you get back."

"What do you mean by that?"

"Screw you, Wily."

She looked in my direction, and without answering, pointed to the door.

When I got out of her car, Jeannette slid over into the driver's seat, put it in gear and spun out, spitting gravel everywhere. Still, I waved goodbye. She wasn't going to stick around to see if I'd be okay, if I could get it running again.

At that point, the sexual tension we briefly shared a few miles ago began to fade like her beautiful red Firebird on the horizon. I thought we had reached a point where she didn't care if I came back or not. I stood holding the roll of duct tape and a gallon of water; I wasn't sure whether I'd make it back myself. I wasn't sure if it wasn't a permanent breakdown from an overheated drive out there.

Still I wrapped everything connected to the radiator in silver and made it to Reliable. It did end up being a simple hose replacement. Afterward I drove to the Lucky U, went to my room and waited for Jen to call. I'd done this similar routine a hundred times before, but like other experiences, she didn't call. No woman ever called when you hang around waiting for the phone to ring.

Lucy was another lost woman of my past. Since she never turned her phone on except to check for messages, I went by her apartment and then the motel. "Haven't see her since she got back," said Eloy Munn, watching television at the registration desk. "Check at her mother's house."

"Eloy, can I ask you a personal question?"

"If it don't take more than the commercial break. What is it?"

"How'd you come up with the name Lucky U?"

"If you haven't noticed it's shaped like a U. And when I built the place during the boom, people were lucky to have a place to live instead of under a bridge by the river. You satisfied?"

I wasn't until he told me where Lucy's mother lived. When I got there, Jean Munn stood at the door all nice and friendly and told me that Lucy went to Las Vegas for a singing gig and she didn't know where she was staying.

19

The daily routine of working for the *Great Valley Beacon* now was mostly on cruise control, as if life's decisions followed a set pattern laid out in a maze. But I'd begun running into more dead ends than a caged rat. The offer of a free vacation, even to a place like Laughlin, was like putting the week on autopilot.

Initially Jeannette had made it difficult to leave town. First she gave me the silent treatment, refusing to call me at home. Then, through the week there was minimal personal contact or communication at the office. The daily assignments were met, but nobody seemed to care about covering anything of importance except for the vital statistics that occurred on a regular basis, like police reports and bland meetings.

Jen wasn't around much except to put the finishing touches on the paper and website. Rusty was in and out of the office so much he should have installed a revolving door. And Jim Tucker said he was taking some time off. Confidentially, he said, to look for another job.

On Friday morning Jen called me over to her desk and said, "I shouldn't care what you do, you know. Try not to have too good a time without me." She gave me a relaxed smile and proceeded to ignore me, choosing the computer over my presence.

And that was it. No more resistance. Like she didn't care anymore, resigned to the fact that our relationship was drifting apart.

"It's just two nights. It's not as if it's eternity," I reiterated before leaving her.

"Sure, and I'll be here with hugs and kisses anxiously awaiting your return. Until then, I've some work that needs my immediate attention. So if you don't mind . . ."

Jeannette could be menacing at times, a mean streak that defined our differences. She acted like nothing mattered more than her job. Although she thought I was on the verge of going back to Vegas, I was really more committed than ever to keep working with her.

Friday afternoon Jen wasn't around to see me off. Except for the receptionist and the ad manager, everyone had left for the day. Rusty Gates had vanished at noon and took half the production women with him to lunch. Jen also took off early so she could spend the weekend at Lake Powell with her husband and their friends on a boat. At three o'clock I decided to shove off myself.

After packing lightly, I headed toward the Greater Valley Regional Airport to catch the afternoon charter.

I didn't think twice about being airborne over a land I was mostly familiar with on the ground. From above, in the uninterrupted blue openness and bright sun, the arid southwest was a majestic display of spires and cliffs cresting like waves. Between the swales and long dark shadows of the waning day below were clusters of communities, like small islands in a brown Nevada sea. On approach and looking down at Laughlin, the glinting reflection of the late sun rippled off the Colorado River, various windshields and the stark glass facades of a few mammoth hotels.

An hour and a half before that, on the flight out, I sat next to one of the lucky winners of Gates' contest. He was a mechanic at the local Ford dealer and a paramedic. I recognized him as one of the volunteers from the Greater Valley Ambulance and Fire Protection District that came to Derrick Banyan's rescue.

When I introduced myself as the reporter for the *Beacon*, he said his name was Rick Monroe.

"So Rick, what's your biggest request?" I asked with a casual curiosity. The plane had just taken off and I was in a giddy, information-gathering frenzy.

"What do you mean?" he asked.

"What kind of emergencies do you respond to the most?" I was trying not to be patronizing, as I didn't want to scare him from taking the bait. "Just curious about the trials and tribulations of being a rescue worker in the valley, is all."

"Heart attacks. At least during the winter." He was starting to warm up from the chill he no doubt felt sitting next to a reporter.

"No kidding? I figured car accidents," I said, fishing.

"Nope. Cardiac arrest. Luckily there's always new blood or Great Valley might be a ghost town in a few years." He thought himself funny, chuckled a little, then soberly added that the busiest time of the year for heart attacks or other natural deaths was December through March. "Happens across the country, no matter the climate."

"Really?" I acted surprised, but already knew that from the increased number of obits in every newspaper I'd ever worked for.

"Yeah. That can also be true with car accidents, if it's a really bad winter."

"Guess winter can be really hard on people around here."

"That and hunting season. We get all types of injuries."

"So, probably life in general then," I said, taking a moment to turn my head and stare out into blue space as a relief from the uncomfortable craning position of looking sideways while talking to Rick. "It's like you never know when you might be driving along and your car goes flying off the road, you know?" I added, speaking into the Plexiglas window and watching another valley roll by off the port side.

"I guess. We get a lot of cars going off the road. Especially during hunting season."

"What about Derrick Banyan? He did some unintentional off-roading."

"He fell asleep. Pretty common, you know."

"Did you answer the call?" I asked. "Out of curiosity . . ." trying to ease into the situation then quickly added the prerequisite and prosaic remark. "I mean off the record, of course."

He said, "Yeah, I was there."

"I should've been talking to you all along." That seemed to really put the scare into him.

"What do you mean?" He acted slightly surprised. Under the calm demeanor was agitation about to surface. But I kept pressing him since he had no place to go at the moment.

"The cops haven't given me much to go by."

"Everything I read about in the paper is how it happened. For a change you guys finally got it right." He said it with masked irritation. "I don't think there's anything else a person could say."

"But it didn't make much sense. I mean, the guy falls asleep at about eight, a couple of miles from his home?"

"Sure, a little after eight. Happens anytime, especially during hunting season, being tired and all, only they're a thousand miles from their hometown," he said in a brusque manner.

"We're not talking about a hunter or a drunk." I pressed on, running the risk of shutting him down completely. People with even an economy-sized ego actually liked talking to a reporter once they got over the fear of 'being quoted' or hadn't yet learned there wasn't any situation which applied to 'off the record' once the words came out.

"Sometimes all it takes is like being up the night before," he said.

"It was pretty gnarly."

"I suppose. But I wasn't the first on the scene."

"Oh, yeah. Who was, Rick, if you don't mind me asking?"

217

"Blanche Banyan and her assistant, Terry or Theresa something. But if you want any of the details you're gonna have to look it up in the report or call the supervisor on that one. I'm not a spokesman for the ambulance service and they'd probably tan my hide if I said something I shouldn't"

Rick squirmed, uncomfortably confined in a seat way too small for his large frame. He pushed back, yawned, and acted bored. The question had jolted him. As if we'd just passed through a pocket of turbulence causing a sudden drop in conversation.

As usual the guy had clammed up, and then stared at the overhead bin until falling asleep.

20

It was a flight without frills or thrills. After landing I wouldn't see Paramedic Rick again until the return flight. He probably went to the dinner shows and did the sightseeing tour, while I had a dollar hotdog in the casino.

After our airport shuttle arrived at the hotel, I took the prerequisite plunge into the ocean of slot machines, roulette wheels, blackjack, craps and poker tables, while sexy, scantily clothed cocktail waitresses swam in between.

Only an hour passed before it was time for me to pull up stakes. After being down a C-note from craps, I went to check-in. The room, cleaner than my abode at the Lucky U, was still 'basic cheap'. It had a TV, two queen-sized beds and a phone with a red message light that wasn't blinking. I was hoping Jen would have called. She knew we were all at the Moulin with its 800 number plastered all over the full-page ads in the *Beacon*.

I had a couple of drinks and kept listening for the phone to ring. She still hadn't tried to reach me.

And I didn't blame her. For all she knew I was in Laughlin grabbing a morsel from the snatch shack, instead of a drink and the solitary feeling that was really keeping me company. When the phone eventually did ring, it influenced my mood greatly. I had high hopes Jen had finally come to her sending unit, but instead it was Rusty.

"Spiver, let's have a drink in the lounge."

"Sure, just give me a minute to freshen up," I said.

"I'm sure you look just fine the way you are."

"I meant my drink, Hoss." I carelessly replaced the receiver, knocking over my third water glass of scotch in my disillusioned state of affairs. It was obvious I had had enough and needed to move away from the vegetative state I was in, and the flask that was killing my brain cells.

Gates was sitting at the bar, staring down at a poker machine. I yanked a free cocktail coupon from the 'Fun Book' everybody was given at the front desk and ordered a Bloody Mary from a gangly looking bartender.

Rusty looked up when the game was over then polished off his usual Jack on the rocks with a cigar chaser. The glass upturned against his mouth as the brown liquid drained down his gullet. He put the glass down and took a puff off the fat stogie. He knew the bartender by name and ordered another whisky from the guy. "No charge," said Bud the bartender. There was a stack of dollar bills in front of his empty glass. Rusty slid one out of the pile when the drinks arrived.

"You got to keep the help happy. What about you, Spiver, you happy?" asked Gates with all the sincerity of a prostitute. He sucked on the cigar and gave me a sidelong glance, lifted his shoulders and straightened his back causing his chest to protrude – proclaiming the posture of authority, I assumed.

"As a clam in his shell except being down a hundred," I said and smiled.

"I meant at work."

"I'm happy if you are, Hoss."

"What's this thing Jen worries about? Something you're supposed to be working on over the weekend, and that's why she didn't want you to go?" inquired that quizzical mind of Rusty Gates, who was now slouching forward into the padded railing. He inhaled deeply from the cigar, then stubbed it out and stared into the reflection behind the bar. I followed his gaze into the amber-colored mirror; a tainted picture of a casino in dark brown shadows cast by the recessed lighting. Gates seemed transfixed on the slot machines.

"Cops think I might know something about Banyan's death they don't," I said to the diminished view of us in the mirror.

"They do?" asked Rusty with feigned surprise. "Where did they get an idea like that?"

"Long story short, I don't have a clue except the chief picked me up snooping around the accident scene. And he keeps asking a lot of questions and threatening me as if I were withholding evidence."

"Find anything out there besides the cops?"

"Nothing but garbage," I confessed.

Rusty Gates wasn't the kind of guy one automatically confided in, even if he was the head honcho. It was hard telling exactly what side he was on. Consequently, I knew to have a healthy mistrust for a system that constantly burned your ass if you revealed your sources.

"Then, Wily, my man, give it up already. Unless you know something you're not talking about." Rusty polished off his drink and stood to leave. He scooped up the stack of bills, and said: "If there is, I don't want to be the last to find out or I'd consider it an act of insubordination. Fair enough?"

"You got it, Hoss." I smiled again and he walked off with a disgruntled sigh into the bright lights of the casino. Rusty had bigger fish to fry, like a whale of a debt he would try to reduce by shooting the rest of his wad at craps or poker.

I strode through the rainbow of lights and the cacophony of sounds. And within that fanciful spectrum which arched across the room, there might be possibly a pot of gold. However, realistically, I never expected anything out of a casino except a thinner wallet. But I still looked in vain, directly at the cherries, bars and sevens reeling past; fixated in a desultory manner on payoff lines and the possibility of solid alignment. And a cocktail waitress that was serving me another scotch.

At first I experienced a sensory overload from the kaleidoscopic effect of overlapping color schemes and bright flashing lights from the slot machines. Normally, color imbued the senses, brought to life inanimate objects like Christmas trees. But the casino was so dense in color you couldn't see the trees for the forest, an optical reality where everything had dulled and lost any glimmer of distinction except the glowing green felt of the craps table.

What green is to a golfer, tennis or pool player, it was the same hue that attached itself to the retina of the craps shooter. That and white dots on red dice and the chips piled high onto the table. I stayed focused on my small amount of chips at all times except when the dice landed. My view moved from the dice to the chips and back again, trying to calculate the significance of each roll.

In the past I had lost in so many ways, and not necessarily by crapping out, but because of a limited attention span—chips plucked by other players or dealers, payoffs that weren't made, Bloody Marys and any other techniques applied that day to increase the losses.

But then again, that was my life in general. In hindsight, things slipped by which should have been noticed at the time. And like craps, once things were in motion there was no changing course or odds. I returned to my room to regroup.

On the nightstand the telephone's message light flashed. Jen had called, said it was urgent we talk, would call later. Then demanded: "But don't call me, I'm with my husband most of the time on that stinking boat."

I flipped on the tube, poured out the remainder of scotch from the traveling flask, surfed the channels, and wished I'd taken her advice and stayed at home. But what's the difference? Eventually I fell asleep to an intoxicating nightmare of dice that became ice cubes I kept chewing on in front of a craps table. Players in violent moods kept rapping their fists against the tabletop for me to spit it out, but it was actually someone knocking at the door.

"What is it?" I yelled deliriously. I stumbled along the worn path in the purple green carpet and looked through the peephole. It was Gates smiling below his cowboy hat. He had a bottle of Jack Daniels.

I opened up. "Come in, Hoss. What's up?"

"Thought we should share a drink, what do you think? You look like shit."

"Sure. Why not? " I said in a tone with all the sincerity it deserved.

"Take it easy, will you, Wily? Relax. Don't get bent. He flipped on the fluorescent light above the bathroom sink in search of another water glass.

Gates' rambling had nothing to do with anything relevant to my state of mind, but instead he wanted to borrow some cash.

I looked at the phone, tried to imagine Jen's urgency while Rusty poured out two cube-less drinks and stood before the television, flipping through the stations until stopping on some indoor motocross event. He studied it as if he had a bet on the outcome. The race could last forever with my luck.

"Here, have another drink. Listen, Spiver, I need a small loan." He acted like I didn't have a choice, as if I owed him the pleasure, while I held out my glass. "You're all right with that, aren't you? 'Bout a grand ought to do it."

I'd only brought $800 cash with about $700 left after an hour at the tables and slots. It wouldn't last more than another two hours at that rate. I needed to pace myself a little, and I hoped half that amount would satisfy the craving. "I'm down cash already; how about two?"

He laughed and poured another shot of Jack into my glass next to the phone. He hovered above me as I sat on the bed. Then he paced back toward the television. "It's just until we get back. Snag a couple of cash advances off the credit card and we're back in business."

"What's that supposed to mean?"

"Look at it as if your future depended on it." He laughed some more, poured whiskey and lit a Camel. "Where's the ashtray?"

"On the table in front of you." I was exasperated at the guessing game. "What future we talking about?"

"The paper. I used part of the *Beacon* as collateral in a poker game and need help getting it back. How much can you scrape together, you think? A grand would be nice, but two's better than one."

Credit cards always meant short-term pleasures with long-term commitments. I had them for that reason. I didn't want a lasting relationship. Just a certain quality of life, which was hard to maintain in moments like these.

I wouldn't see the money again. But I had to bet on Rusty anyway, if not for me then Jen. I looked at the phone and wondered if she sensed my not wanting her to call.

Gates sat at the little round table, transfixed on the motocross race, avoiding any further discussion. He was ready to hit the casino's ATM.

"Ready to hit the road, Jack?" Rusty asked the bottle in his hand.

"Where's the game?"

"Up on ten with some old Laughlin buddies, currently fifty-one percent your boss."

"Have you talked to Jen about the new hierarchy?" It wasn't such a long shot thinking this related to Jen's need to talk. Better than her desperately missing me when Rusty was in the room.

"Briefly. Want to keep the help happily informed. Now, Wily, I'm on the move. Don't mind if we cruise on down now, do you?"

I was getting exasperated with him and it was starting to show. "Not until you tell me what Jen had to say about losing the paper."

"Chill out. So you've been hosing the help, Spiver?" He laughed to try and get me off his back. "But hey, I really don't want to know and don't care about your personal affairs."

That shut me up and any desire to discuss the day's events with Jen was left behind in the room. Rusty filled the void though. He pushed me along and unknowingly offered protection from any assault from weirdoes lurking anywhere.

Rusty was only around long enough to get the five hundred I managed to scrape together, leaving me with the few remaining twenties. I wandered among the twenty-five cent slots, stuck in a bill and pulled at a quick fix.

The wheels spun, symbols clicked in place and nothing but a few credits remained. I was too short for craps. Everything seemed hopeless until three sevens in red, white and blue lined up. A jackpot of credits appeared on the meter.

After cashing in, I moved down the row of machines winning another five hundred credits. One hundred twenty five in raw form. The machine made noise for my listening pleasure, so I played more, pushing the 'Bet All' button maniacally, not wasting any time on the one arm. A cocktail waitress started coming around more frequently. And time dissipated like exhaled smoke. I was dissolutely adrift in the chaotic sea of mechanical madness.

It was a good run, but didn't last. Back in the room around eleven-thirty, there were two terse messages from Jeannette wondering where the hell I was. Again with the urgency, but nothing could be done except wait patiently. I had a strong feeling of detachment, the disconnection as destiny, and if she tried again, something would prevent us from talking.

As if on cue, there was a knock at the door. It was Rusty again. He came in and sat at the table, but I was about tapped out. I told him, "Whatever remaining credit I have I figure I'll need to live on until the next job."

"Spiver, you're gainfully employed. I'm still the man in charge. I'm doing good at the break. Got a little time before it starts up."

"I couldn't withdraw any more money even if I wanted to."

"Sure you can. It's after midnight." He referred to the ATM's internal clock, limiting withdrawals in a twenty-four hour period. So, we could repeat the whole process again. "You got anything to drink?" said Rusty, who had picked up the remote and flipped on the tube.

"Not anymore."

"Then let's hit the bar, what do you say?" He was jittery, jumped up and paced along the same worn path. He'd walk toward the door as if to leave, halted, turned around and headed to the heavily draped window and circular table and chair, deciding whether or not to sit, then cocked his head with a question. "You ready?"

"Sure." I wasn't, but the bar sounded like an acceptable distraction.

Rusty recognized two gorgeous, scantily clothed cocktail waitresses. The women stood talking at the end of the bar where the service area was. They clutched their round serving trays and waved.

We sat in a dark corner booth. Rusty stared in the direction of the waitress at the bar. "Mighty fine, Wily," he said, then repeated "mighty fine" for emphasis. I couldn't tell if he was angling for her or making conversation, trying to ease into what he really wanted. "With the right amount of cash a man can just about have anything his lil 'ol heart desires."

Turned out he knew the waitress who squinted into the darkness, searching for someone in need of a drink in our corner, or for some kind of romance in mind.

At that point, talking to Rusty was like trying to shift gears with a broken transmission. Nothing but a stall position. Finally, "You two old friends?" I asked since he hadn't talked in about five minutes.

"Never seen her before in my life."

Liar, I thought.

She came with all smiles, moved slowly around the lounge looking as if to serve its sparse customer base, eventually heading in our direction.

"Rusty, you ole hound dog!" She greeted him with enthusiasm. "You're back so soon."

"Couldn't turn down the possibilities of us hooking up again. What's it been?" Rusty couldn't remember. "How 'bout a couple of Jacks, help me remember the good times we had? And by the way," he added, "What are you and that lovely woman doing after work tonight?" He looked deep in the valley of her cleavage as she bent over to kiss him on the cheek.

"Heading home, I reckon," she said, still smiling away. "We're trailer mates over in Bullhead City." She indicated the other waitress. "You guys staying here at the hotel?"

"Sure are. How 'bout the two of you joining us for a drink when you get off," said Rusty, pointing to the waitress who started wiping down tables.

"Hey, Laura, they're wondering if we want to join them for a drink afterwards," Rusty's friend shouted to the other waitress.

"Don't get off until two," Laura said while picking up a tray full of empty glasses off a table and then walking in our direction to get a better look at who was interested. She seemed a little apprehensive before adding, "Sure, why not?"

Rusty introduced me to his Laughlin girlfriend, Elaine, and her friend Laura.

"See you around two," said Elaine while giving Rusty the sly eye as to her intentions. "Rusty, I need to ask a favor but it'll wait 'til later." She wasn't the only one. People started to line up like a pileup at rush hour wanting him.

"Anything for you, sweetheart." Rusty Gates gleamed. "I need to do a little catching up, too. Now how about two more?" Rusty almost pleaded, "Wily, *you old hound dog*, I need a couple of C-notes. Should have it back before you know what's missing."

Rusty was starting to piss me off. He grinned and his smoke filled my air space. Cigarettes and unlucky strikes on my credit accounts were enough to make anyone nauseous. And all I did was sit back, down my whiskey and take it like a sap. Because beyond the games there's an incalculable debauchery in any gambling town that made making a loan to Rusty Gates seem like a relatively safe investment.

I wanted to go back to the room. Maybe Jen would call. I'd let her know she was right about what a mistake Laughlin had been. So I said to Rusty, "Hey, Hoss, what about calling it a night, instead?"

"Not on your life, old buddy. I got the mojo working. I can feel it."

We drank, tipped heavily and waved our goodbyes to Elaine and Laura, who stood at the corner of the bar expecting our return.

I gave him some of my winnings from the slot machine, then went up to my room and stretched out on top of what felt like a rental truck blanket. It made me feel like I was packed and ready for shipment to Jeannette in a box addressed to her husband. When the phone rang, I sprang to life like a jackass-in-the-box.

"Yo, partner, it's two a.m. and we got some hot little honeys to wrangle with. We're at the bar so get your ass on down," Gates yelled into the receiver. "By the way, you talk to Jen lately?"

That snapped me to attention. "No, why?"

"Just curious. You coming?"

"Give me a few." I thought Rusty must have been on the same wavelength, mentioning Jen. And then after a cool shower the phone rang again. I traipsed across the room, trailing water, and it stopped. I toweled off and began dressing when I caught the red light flashing a message. It was Jen, whispering, "So, you're still out carousing. Don't blow the whole bankroll. Got some news. I'll try and reach you later; it's important we talk."

Rusty, Elaine and Laura were sitting in the same corner booth of the lounge. On the table were several bottles of beer. I sat next to Laura. She handed me one and said, "It may be warm by now. I ordered it about twenty minutes ago."

"Hey, buddy, it's about time," Rusty said over the pop rock band playing on stage.

"Let's dance, Rusty," said Elaine. They were definitely a cowboy couple. She had the look of hearty Midwest stock, tall with long blonde curls. Always laughing a lot, drinking beer and looking like the life of the party. She stood and tugged on his shirtsleeve, urging him out of the seat's deep cushion. And off they went, leaving us alone.

"How long have you two known each other?" I asked Laura.

"I've known Rusty ever since I decided to come to Laughlin. Oh, 'bout a year, I'd guess."

"Old friends?"

"Old enough to be my father. Just kidding. We're just mutual friends. Elaine's got the hots for him, though.

"So how's Laughlin been treating you?" I yelled, trying to make myself heard. She looked over thirty, scrawny, with frizzy red hair and frown lines along her cheeks. But she was probably in her late twenties, just with ravaged features from living the hard life as a hooker.

She shrugged and mouthed the word "Rough." She was making eye contact with the beer bottle she held with both hands and peeled away at the corners of the label. When the band finished its love song, she continued. "I met a guy. We got married. Come to find out he was the jealous type who took out his aggression on his wife. I guess it was the marriage I wanted and not him. I was a working girl in Vegas at the time."

"That can put a strain on any relationship. Sorry, I don't know what to say."

She laughed, then pouted. "It's crazy, I know. It really had more to do with my ex." She stared down at the bottle of Bud and continued to scrape with her thumbnails. Tiny pieces of red and white paper scattered about. I absently looked in the direction of Rusty and Elaine walking back from the dance floor.

"Got busted a couple of times hooking in Vegas and he would bail me out. So I became indebted to him. So much for free enterprise.

"So why live in Laughlin?"

"Vegas got too crazy, and I wanted to get away from the ex."

Rusty and Elaine sat down dripping sweat and Laura changed the subject. "I moved to Bullhead City, just across the river. It's where a lot of Laughlin's working class live. It reminds me of back

232

home over there. You boys ought to come over. Bet you never been to Bullhead; well, have you?"

I was pretty sure Rusty knew it well. Judging by the way he was lit, it must have been the invitation he was looking for.

21

As was his style, Rusty had said he didn't like riding in an airport shuttle. Way too camp. So he had rented the biggest upgrade the agency had in stock. The Lincoln Town Car fit him handsomely. Ninety percent of the time the car rested in the sweltering blacktop parking lot of the Moulin Casino and Hotel. One of its two big trips with Rusty and me was across the river to Bullhead City, following a beat-up Chevy Cavalier.

It wasn't a forced situation, but there was a clear understanding with Rusty of the circumstances under which I had agreed to go with him. He was driven by an erotic impulse and Elaine wasn't going to let him act on it unless I went along, too. Red taillights led us through the desert blackness as nocturnal creatures receded from our headlights.

We finally reached their gray trailer on the outskirts of Bullhead. Laura parked and we pulled up alongside. Rusty got of the car and closed ranks between him and Elaine, grabbing her waist. She hung around Rusty's neck for a support hug, drawing him closer to her lips for a kiss.

Something was up besides Rusty's dick. Nothing felt right about the scene. Elaine, doing a listing crab-walk, led the way up the wooden stairs. She swung open the battered metal door and yelled, "Here, doggie, doggie. Come to mama." Her raspy voice filled the tin cavern, "look-a-what the cat brought home." She leaned into the doorway, and pulled open the handle until the top became unhinged.

A rumbling sound came from the shadows and out stepped Jimmy. "What the hell did you do to the door?" he said with the flick of a switch that transformed everything into a more acceptable reality. The coffee table was cluttered with beer cans, the sofa cushions had guts oozing out. "It's goddamn three. What ya doing disturbing my peace for?" He stood shirtless, in tight jeans that pushed his body's frame upward in a mass of flabby flesh with thick, hairy arms.

Elaine turned off the fluorescent tubes above and switched on a lava lamp. A burnt orange glow illuminated the room. She slinked from the living room to the kitchen area that was divided by a counter. After pulling a bottle of vodka off the fridge, she found glasses by the sink and grabbed an orange pitcher from the ice box. Then setting everything down on the counter like a bartender tending bar, she said, "Screwdriver anyone? I got ice in the freeze if you need it."

"Jimmy, meet Wily. Rusty you already know. How 'bout joining us for a little breakfast?" Elaine said. Rusty stared hard at Jimmy and didn't say a word.

"Damn it," Jimmy shouted. "If you weren't family, I'd a half beat ya by now for ripping the fucking door off the hinges again."

Elaine was demanding: "Shut up already with the door, you fucking oaf," then stabbed a knife into the orange juice pitcher and stirred.

"A screwdriver, Wily? How about you, Laura?"

Everyone agreed to one. And Rusty and Elaine sat on the sofa, embraced in each other's arms, kissing. Jimmy staggered back down the hall hole he had crawled out of, muttering some kind of threat. Laura and I sat on bar stools at the counter.

A quick screw was what Rusty was angling for and didn't need to announce it orally. Instead, he got up on Elaine's urging and headed down the hall. I went and sat in a severely wounded chair: a broken spring poking hard in my ass.

"Here," said Laura, handing me one of the two drinks Elaine had made. She moved to the couch. "Sit over here, unless you like the feel of that anal probe."

"Not particularly." I sat next to her and found a spot on the coffee table among the empty beer bottles to put my drink.

Laura inched closer and put her arm along my back, grabbing me by the shoulder. "Hope it's not too strong for you."

"The drink, you mean?"

"Yeah, the drink. What, am I coming on too strong?" she said and smiled and pulled her hair back into a ponytail. "So what are you thinking? Don't worry. I won't bite unless you want me to."

"So where'd you and Elaine work together in Vegas?" I said.

"The Depot. One of those chains that NRI owns. Why?"

"Ever heard of a guy named Victor Saville?"

"Sure. He's one of the big wigs there. That and Sid's."

She took a sip off her drink, and then drained everything but the ice.

"Drink up. You want another?" she said, towering above me after abruptly standing up.

"Not yet." Then I drained the glass and changed my mind and added, "Sure, why not?"

Laura went around the counter and mixed two more screwdrivers. We drank to old friends. And I asked her, "So what do you know about Victor Saville?"

"What?" She was in the process of taking another sip — "Oh, he's part of some group out of Nevada."

After yet another swig of the sweet orange swill, I prodded on: "You ever met him?"

"Just in passing. Why the questions?"

"It's the reporter in me. I used to work for a guy named Rudy Morris."

"Good old Rudy. He used to shoot me for those escort ads."

"I know the ones," I admitted. "A while back I did the copywriting but I don't remember seeing you in there."

"I wasn't there very long," she said. "How about we talk about something else tonight as long as there's chemistry between us?"

I was holding my drink in my left hand when she reached over and pulled at my belt before losing her grip and falling backward onto the coffee table, slumping to the floor.

"Ouch. That *fucking* hurt." She grimaced at the scattered cans and bottles. I quickly leaned forward and grabbed her arms and pulled.

"You all right?" I said. "Here, how about another cocktail?" But it was too late. The tipped vodka drink had created a toxic spill. "Oh shit, looks like another dead soldier."

"I'm okay. Here, I'll get some beer from the fridge." Laura stood up, rubbed her head and wandered sideways into the kitchen. A hint of sun began to bleed through the gray of the trailer's innards, as sounds of human rummaging came from the back bedroom followed by Rusty's emergence..

"What the hell is going on?" Rusty said from the hallway, tucking his shirt into his jeans. He wobbled on the heels of his cowboy boots. "You ready? He asked me in a barely audible voice. "Let's hit the road."

I agreed. "Looks like we're outta here," I yelled to Laura and followed Rusty toward the door.

As Rusty drove, Saturday morning's sun rose like the blob in Elaine's lava lamp. The blazing light manifested itself into a burning headache. When we finally pulled up to The Moulin, I could barely remember Jen had called.

Among her many attributes, Jeannette was very intuitive, smart, suspicious, and even skeptical. If I were fortunate enough, she would be jealous without the rage in her countenance. But the phone never rang and any need for explanation was lost in the last thing I remembered looking at, the ceiling.

It was after one the following afternoon when someone banged on the door, ignoring the plea hanging on the knob not to be disturbed. But someone was yelling anyway. "Maid service" she repeated and banged on the door until I opened it and said to the woman in jeans and a halter top. "What's this, you clean rooms too?"

"Hey, sweetheart. I came by to give you a little jump start." It was Laura.

"I'm beyond charging." I stood in the doorway in a tee shirt and underwear, no doubt looking as haggard as I felt.

"Bullshit. You look horrid." She passed through the door waving a little amber vial hanging from a tiny silver spoon. "I got just the thing for what ails you."

The sight of the vile of white stuff produced deep-seated memories of anxiety and depression, which flashed before my eyes like a hypnotic stupor. It had been over a decade since I tried that awful shit. With an exaggerated yawn, I tried to infer the only cure was crashing big time. "Laura, I'm completely wiped out," I said, but she sprawled out on the bed anyway.

"You wanna know about Vic the Dick and I got something to tell."

My curiosity was slightly sparked since I hadn't totally burned out.

"Come here," she said. "I need your help. It would mean a lot."

"If it's cash, I'm stretched to hell. Ask Rusty."

239

Laura said, "It's not about money. But it never hurts to have a little security."

"Aren't you glad we didn't get married? I would have been a poor provider."

She didn't want an answer, but told me instead, "That's why it was strictly business with Rusty. But to his credit, he was the least offensive guy I'd met after coming here. He really had a thing for me, but love isn't some monogamous walk up the aisle."

"I have a feeling you don't know him like I do," I said half jokingly.

I walked to the edge of the bed and stood above her. She was on her back and let out a laugh. She slid her hand up my leg and under my underwear, and was disappointed.

"I can't mess around, but it's not because you aren't an object of desire," I said and backed up. It was true. She was the kind Hustler Magazine dreams were made of.

"Shit, don't give me that," she demanded. "But if you can't . . . ."

"It's that I've got a girlfriend and she might not appreciate the situation."

"I thought you were kind of interested last night. So what's the hold up, or let down in your case? You want to or not?"

"Without a doubt, but I can't."

" . . . Fuck?" The single word expressed the whole spectral feeling instead of long convoluted phrases which beat around the bush. She slid out of her halter-top and jeans, and slid under the rumpled sheets. "Let's talk. Maybe do a line," she said.

I expected the phone to ring. Any moment. I could sense it. Any moment, repeated the thought loop.

But Jeannette didn't call. The state of denial ebbed into a hard time of maintaining control.

"Help yourself to a line instead," she insisted.

"I wouldn't, under normal circumstances, but I'm feeling a little puny."

"Looks like things are beginning to feel a little perky."

"It's an emotional reaction."

"Go ahead, big boy." Her laugh had a shrill whine at the end. It stuck out in bad form along with other lewd thoughts.

I stood before the giant mirror above the credenza with a Franklin up my nose. It was a portrait of a disheveled reporter mired in a bleak landscape of tawdry surroundings. And there was Laura, back against the headboard and draped below the neck in a rippling white sheet that looked a lot like a wedding dress.

I said, "Shit, I can't do this crap." And put the cap back on the vial and the bill in the wallet. Then the phone rang. At the same time there was a knock at the door. "What the hell's going on?" I thought out loud.

Laura shrieked, "It's Rusty at the door and your girlfriend on the phone."

"You're pretty perceptive." I rushed to grab my jeans on the chair. Pulled them on and yelled at the door, "Wait a minute."

"Who else are you expecting? I guess it's a strong possibility my ex followed me here. He's been stalking me since we divorced." A worrisome look

241

crept into Laura's expression. She pulled away the sheet and quickly dressed.

"Who's there?" I yelled at the door, as if I didn't already know.

"Who do you think, the bogeyman? Open up."

When I did, Rusty stepped inside the room, smiling. "Yo, what's shaking?" I thought I heard him say, but wasn't sure since the phone was still ringing, mixing words with emotions. Rusty followed me into the room as I went to answer it. Jeannette was on the line while I sat on the sideline watching Rusty and Laura get reacquainted.

Jen happily greeted me with: "Finally!"

"I knew you'd call eventually." It was 1:32. From the scrambled numbers emerged a sense of panic, and in an affected tone I added, "I thought it would have been sooner than . . ." I stuttered on, "than now."

"Who's there, Wily?" demanded Jeannette. "Catch you at a bad time?" She had started to sound testy at that point.

"Not at all. It's Rusty and a friend of his. How are you? Perturbed or peaceful, I can't be sure."

"I'm fine. I got some news but it can wait until you are alone. You sound out of it, though."

"All those euphoric moments at the casino start to add up. How's the lake?"

"Hot. There's hardly any water left. And the marina is a mud hole. What's up with Rusty and his little entourage?"

Rusty broke the line of questioning and asked if it was Jen. "Let me talk to her."

I said to Jen, "Did you hear? Rusty wants to talk to you."

242

"I heard. I need to talk to him, too."

"But your message last night sounded urgent," I said.

"Tell you later. Now put Rusty on."

Rusty moved to the adjacent bed, lit a cigarette, and grabbed the receiver. He watched Laura intently and sighed at the sight of her heading for the chair. " . . . I don't know, a couple friends we hooked up with last night," he was telling Jen. A long pause followed, penetrating the room like noxious gases. "I don't know. I just got here when you called. Why don't you ask him?"

The excuses I wanted to tell Jen as to why I had a woman in the room became as twisted as the coiled phone cord. But Rusty hung up before I had a chance to say anything.

"She's pissed," said Rusty and inhaled deeply. "What's going on with you and Laura?"

"She stopped by is all. What's happening with Jen?"

"Something about taxes. I'll tell you later." I studied Rusty for a reaction.

Laura bummed a cigarette from Rusty, blew smoke all over the room, then stubbed it out.

22

There was something odd, out of place and even suspicious among the natural surrounding of black asphalt and vehicles in the parking lot. Under the fierce sun, a pickup truck idled with a laborious engine moan unlike its parked counterparts. Dark tinted windows made it virtually impossible to see who was doing what inside; perhaps spying on the Moulin and its parking garage across the street or on some sort of liaison with a hotel maid. Who knew? But without the AC running it would have been an oven and easily baking anyone inside.

Rusty and I noticed it as we crossed the street and headed toward the bank for one last withdrawal. Laura stayed behind in the room to sleep off the remnants of the night before.

"What the hell do you think is going on in there?" I asked Rusty about the anomaly.

"Somebody trying to commit suicide," he said from under the brim of his cowboy hat. He had been flipping through his wallet and wasn't paying much attention when a rough looking hick emerged from the truck. The strange ranger was the intimidating size of six-five, beard and straw hat, adding another six inches to the massive frame.

"Hey, I need to talk to you boys," he yelled, waving us over.

"What's that prick want?" Rusty was finally agitated at something other than a cash shortage.

"He doesn't look like your typical panhandler."

"Good, I got nothing to give him except a broken jaw if he asks." Rusty's agitation turned to curiosity and he added, "Let's see what he wants."

As we approached the rear of the truck, it was easy to make out the outline of a rifle on the gun rack through the tinted back window. It seemed normal enough in these parts, unless the bastard decided to point it as us. Rusty made that maneuver impossible though, backing the guy up enough to block the driver's door. I stood alongside Rusty, temporarily blocking traffic until we moved onto the sidewalk.

"I'm looking for Laura. She's not at work, but her car's here. I need to know, you guys seen her lately?" He pulled off his sunglasses and squinted directly at Gates.

"Not lately," said Rusty, who was looking to keep it brief.

"What do you want with Laura?" I said and put sunglasses on to lessen a harsh glare.

The brawny bastard leered forward in his boots, pointing a finger in my chest before Rusty blinded-sided him. The fist-to-face blow staggered him slightly, and then as the guy wobbled from side to side, Rusty kneed him in the gut for good measure. The guy stumbled in a small semicircle, nearly collapsing before regaining composure. He rubbed the left side of his face and said, "Fuck you, asshole. That wasn't necessary."

"I've had about enough of this kind of hospitality." Rusty stood in the guy's tracks, ready to pop him again, and said: "Who the fuck are you, anyway?"

"Back off, asshole. It's Laura I want." The guy pointed at me and said: "Next time it's your fucking ass in a sling."

It wasn't the threat that was bothersome but a fear tracing through my mind as I contemplated my sanity for revisiting the dim reaches of Nevada. The guy got in his truck, and squealed away without looking, almost sideswiping a shiny red Cadillac.

It was comical to a point, except the guy was a menace of sorts. Rusty chuckled anyway while flexing his hand, making sure it was still in working order. "What the hell was that fool on, PCP? I really wanted to crack him good, but it's not worth the risk."

"It's Laura's ex-husband, I think." As we continued walking toward the bank, I added, "He's really the possessive type. Laura says he's been stalking her since her divorce."

Gates was smiling at the sight of the Nevada National Bank sign half a block away, as if his only concern was a teller for more money than an ATM would dispense. We headed back to the hotel. I grabbed the elevator and went to the room.

Looking for Laura was like looking for the secret passage in a vanishing act at a magic show. When I opened the door no one was there except a note saying she and Elaine had left for Vegas.

246

But what I really wanted to see was the red light flashing, and it was. But, instead of Jeannette it was Lucy saying she went to Sid's City and had given the Smart Phone to Victor Saville as a favor. That he'd know what to do with it. And I would know everything I wanted to find out.

"Wily," she said in the voice mail, "I called Jeannette to find out where you were staying and she said that it was good that I called today because tomorrow the phone was going to be disconnected and the paper seized for delinquent taxes. And I could have you because she was leaving town to live with her aunt in Crescent City."

* * *

Rusty was at the bar when I walked in. He had won at poker and was into celebrating. "Drinks on me," said Rusty and began counting out the money I'd loaned him. "Here's your lucky money. Try the middle table. The ice is on fire."

I said, "Laura and Elaine went to Vegas."

"I know. Elaine called. I'm going to pick her up tonight. Laura's staying in Vegas and doesn't want her ex to know where she's going to be living."

"You mind if I ride along? Lucy Branch is working at Sid's City and I need to hook up with her. She's got a cell phone for me."

"About time you got another phone. It's been a pain in the ass tracking you down."

"It's not mine. Lucy found it at the crash site where Derrick Banyan went off the road. I don't know whose it is, but she gave it to Victor Saville.

He'll probably be able to find the owner without a problem.

Rusty was full of suspicion. "Why Saville?"

"Because he'll know people who can retrieve information from it. See who owns it. Hopefully there's a story there. That is if there's a paper around to print it."

"I guess we'll see when you get back. But I don't have a good feeling about it. How come you didn't tell me about the phone sooner?" he said.

"After Lucy found it, she went back to Vegas before I had a chance to get it from her. The battery was dead so there was no way to tell whose it was anyway. Besides, what was I going to do with a phone that was probably encrypted?"

Before we could leave, Rusty wanted to finish his run at the tables.

* * *

Pythagoras, considered the first mathematician, believed everything could be represented in numbers, and numbers symbolized spiritual entities whose presence is felt in all existence. Others believed that numbers vibrate and have distinct energy patterns.

That night there were all sorts of vibes. I took some cash and headed for the green felt table. Six young beefy jocks stood with their women around the edge ah-hoot'n and ah-holler'n wildly with each roll of the dice. You could feel the heat since the table hadn't gone completely cold yet. I stood along the curved rail and laid down a hundred. Got chips and after the come out roll, I bet on point numbers 4-

5-6-8-9 and a couple of crappy bets on 30-to-1 hardways.

The big hit was on the double six, and immediately I collected about $150; then let everything ride and covered all the hardways. A big busty blonde leaned over the table revealing cleavage a person could get lost in, rolled a double four, paying 10-to-1 plus the point number. After ten rolls with the lucky shooter, I had racked up over $900. A few shooters later scored a two grand total.

The stickman pushed the red cubes my way. I selected two and threw hard for the desired bounce for a 7. Around the perimeter the crowd grew even bigger. I always bet on myself. Gripping the dice and tossing everything into the wind. I threw three point numbers before crapping out and walked away a happy man.

Rusty emerged from the spectators around the table. He was buzzing with enthusiasm. He congratulated me with, "Good job, partner."

And off we drove to Vegas, and Sid's City in particular, where we might find Lucy and Elaine before sunrise. Rusty liked the idea and drove fast.

Rusty disengaged the Town Car's cruise control when he pulled into Vegas around three o'clock. We made our way down the Strip. Rusty flipped off the AC and rolled down all the windows. Warmth flooded in off the familiar kaleido-street. Passing the Circus Circus RV Park brought back memories and all the nightmares that went with living in an aluminum sweatbox with my sweetheart.

We whipped into Sid's City without much fanfare. The valet let out a yawn and accepted the keys to the luxury liner Rusty had pushed beyond the rational speed limits. Gates had raged across the black and empty space beyond Laughlin at an average of 120. Oncoming car lights were like streaking meteors in our path. We had covered the distance in record time and now faced the glittering galaxy of Sid's City.

I went into the lounge to find Lucy but the band was on break, so I had Saville paged to the front desk. We paced the beige marble tiles for fifteen minutes before Saville slid from between gold-mirrored elevator doors. His demeanor spread across the bright marble lobby like a dark shadow as the help flickered to attention and greeted him with feigned pleasantries. It was a relief to see the Crown Vic, otherwise it could have been a wasted trip.

"What can I do for you boys this time of morning?" Saville smiled deviously, approached and shook hands with Gates and me. "You might want to check the action in the poker suite. Rusty, take my place at the table if you want. Although, I have to admit surprise at the sight of you two."

"Spiver is looking for Lucy and thought you might know where she is," Rusty said.

He paused to glance at his watch and retrieved a cigarette from his beige shirt pocket. "Lucy's working. I'm surprised at you, Spiver. What makes you want to piss off someone like me, huh? Start a pissing match that nobody, and I mean *nobody*, wants."

"Vic, as you probably already know, I made a big mistake," I said.

Saville smiled at the discomfort I was feeling and left it at that. All movement around us had moved on. The hotel's lobby was empty. "Lucy has the phone, but I had my boys look into it before I gave it back to her. You might find it interesting, too. I'll let her tell you all about it.'

"Thanks, and sorry about any misunderstandings we had."

"It's a good thing Lucy is on your side. Now, Gates, what the fuck's this about not paying your taxes."

Rusty said, "Can we talk about it over cards?"

I told Rusty I'd be at the bar after he got cleaned out, then went to the lounge hoping to see Lucy. The band was still on break, but I ordered a scotch on the rocks from the joyless bartender, his gaunt features embedded on the video poker machine's glass top. A full house was featured as the cards a person wanted. But it also said GAME OVER superimposed on the screen until twenty bucks worth of five-card stud started the action. With all the zeal of a push-button addict I gambled until the last of the credits.

"Vic said I'd find you down here." It was Lucy looking fabulous. She sat on the barstool next to mine and swiveled to face me. "Any luck?" She was smiling, eyes shinning in the glow of a blue screen. "I've missed you, despite all of the shit that's happened lately between us."

"I've missed you too. And no luck yet. Video poker has never been my strong suit."

"I meant any luck talking to Vic," she said.

"He said to talk to you." Her gaze was soft and for the first time in a while I felt lonely. "Why did you run off so suddenly without telling me?"

"Vic called and wanted me to come out to Vegas immediately. Wily, we need to talk but I've got to get back to work. The band is getting ready."

23

While I waited for Lucy to take another break I went walking along the Strip. Only on a Las Vegas street corner at three in the morning can you find someone selling shoelaces that never need tying. I stared in disbelief at the small gathering that formed a semicircle around the vendor's cart. If anything, I needed to untie the ties that bind. To unwind, I had taken a walk north along the Strip past the Sahara.

A hot desert wind blew in from the west. A few lighted palm trees along the lower end of the Strip swayed like striptease dancers among the neon signs. At the base of their trunks stood the peddlers of porn and escort services. I looked for a copy of Rudy Morris' *Vegas Vanity*, eventually finding one in the hands of a haggard woman street-hawker. Of all the gorgeous gals, not one was recognizable from the past. No doubt they had all moved on, but I stood still, looked and read the scintillating verses of eroticism anyway.

The expected protocol, when I worked for Rudy Morris, was to copy his style verbatim. Although I had learned the difference between an adjective and a noun, sometimes the distinction was lost in the syntax. Rudy's method wasn't based on some English tutorial, but on a vocational instruction book of how to please life's seedy undercurrent in concise prose.

You could take it only so far, though. There wasn't a need to incorporate Morris' style beyond *Vegas Vanity*, where only its readers could appreciate the superfluous decadence brought to life with flesh-colored photos. Working for Morris was more about catering to the demented desires of a voyeur than worrying about proper nouns.

Below an ad for "Rosie's special delivery service, at the bottom of page 2, was the editorial and advertising numbers for Morris Publications. I should have called, let Morris know another payment was available. However, it was way too early. I'd be back in Laughlin by the time anyone was around his office to answer phones. I tossed the magazine in the trash and headed back to Sid's City in search of Rusty Gates.

Rusty was an easy find, hunched over a video poker machine at the bar, sipping a drink with Elaine. They seemed happy at my appearance. Rusty greeted me with, "It's about time. I've been looking all over the place. Let's roll."

"Hey. Have you had the chance to check out the show?"

"She's dine-o-mite," said Elaine. And Rusty agreed.

In between songs, I walked over to the stage and told Lucy that we had to leave in order to get back to Laughlin in time for the flight back. She told the band she needed a couple minutes, then we sat at an empty table near the stage.

"I know you have to go. Here's the phone. It was Blanche's, and has a lot of info on it that Saville was able to retrieve. Some of it was from voice mails, apps and financial statements. She had a lot to gain by Derrick's death. One of the horticulture apps has a bookmark on various poisonous plants that don't leave a trace in the blood. It's kind of like what you always suspected about her all along."

"Wouldn't have known it without you. We make a hell of a team, don't we?" It was more in jest when I said it, but she seemed to like the idea.

"Give me a call when you get back and I'll tell you everything you want to know and then some." She gave me a long kiss then said, "Come back when you can stay awhile longer."

* * *

We headed wearily down the road toward Laughlin. Elaine and Rusty were in the front and I was in the back. I had fallen asleep to a gray dawn until a noise, loud and startling, sent a shock to the glassy surface my thoughts had rested against. Whatever the dreamscape was it shattered into fragments as my head banged even harder on the window the second and third times. Rusty had veered off the highway then back on again. I wasn't sure if it was intentional or if he had also nodded off. He looked just as stupefied as ever.

"What the hell's going on?" I blurted out in delirium.

"A little wake up call," said Rusty. He massaged his eyes with his right fingers, then squinted ahead into the brightening sky.

"Jesus, I think I dreamed we were history."

He gave me a backward glance. "You need to be awake anyway so you can tell me what happened back there." He looked dead serious, flexed his arm and aimed his thumb at the rear window like a hitchhiker. I knew he meant Vegas but I turned around anyhow and saw the self-induced dust storm behind us.

"You sure that maneuver was on purpose?" I asked in disbelief, watching the cloud produced by the Lincoln dissipate into a gust of air.

"Nothing's for sure, you know? Expect that we'll make it back to Laughlin without a scratch. There's a noon flight that you need to make. We were only halfway there so Rusty picked up the speed to ninety. I asked him if he was okay to drive.

"Oh yeah." Rusty lit a cigarette and cracked the window. The grating sound of road wind rushed in. All I could do was release a series of sighs as we drove through a landscape with little vegetation. The inertia of brown dirt and gray sky was a linear pictorial of Nevada, with little representation of humanity except the metal towers connected by power lines strung across the panorama.

Rusty said, "So when I was talking to Saville, he told me about the phone and how much money Blanche was worth. Millions he said. That since she's the sole heir, she owns about half the county. He also told me that gambling ain't happening and that they are pulling out of the Sorrow Creek deal. But I guess you were right, and that I was probably a little over optimistic and should have seen that coming. I was so close to making it happen—you know, the big payoff, but I got blindsided. Jen wanted us to run voter polls but I wouldn't let her."

Quixotica, Man de la Mancha, sadly crossed my mind. I looked over at Rusty, the Don himself, endlessly searching for false ideals and hopes just the other side of Death Valley. Yet he wasn't the only one out swinging a lance at desert mirages.

"What are you looking at?" The question shook me out of my reverie.

"Windmills, a little while ago."

The response took him by surprise. "What the hell you talking about?"

"Don't you think those towers of power are like the windmills from Don Quixote."

"In your dreams, pal. If that's what you mean about Don Quixote."

* * *

Rusty Gates wouldn't give up. No sooner did we enter the Moulin Hotel and Casino than he started plugging away at the slots.

"I'm heading to the room. We have to be checked out by eleven." I yawned and began walking away. I had two hours to pack.

"Hold on," he said and pulled down on the handle. Three sizzling sevens awakened the netherworld after a couple of zombie gamblers drifted by to check the action on his big quarter pay-out.

"A hundred and twenty-five. Not bad for the first couple of pulls." I said between yawns then made my way to the elevators.

Those in the gaming industry—as well as most car dealers—aren't as friendly or as happy as they seem until they have taken you for all you're worth. And I shouldn't expect anything more since it's probably one of the lowest forms of entertainment for the money. Winning is like an unexpected gift, or a free undercoating. Still, there are people like Rusty, who figure they're owed something because they've lost so much. Consequently, I was happy for him.

We ran into each other in the hotel checkout line. He looked tired and frustrated. I knew how haggard he must have felt since I was there also and was about dead on my feet. We both suffered from sleep deprivation. Or was it depravation in general?

"Did you ever get a chance to talk to Jen?" asked Rusty out of the blue.

"No messages, why?"

"I haven't been able to get hold of her. When I called her husband, he said he had the impression she left town. Went to stay with her aunt in Crescent City."

"Yeah, Lucy told me." News of Jen's departure had produced a chilling effect, like being left out in the cold to deal with the insurmountable odds of surviving hypothermia. I had been looking forward to seeing her and then confiding all my feelings of guilt and pain produced by the weekend getaway. I'd held onto an underlying confidence things could be worked out between us.

Yet something was in the air besides the plane I was on.

We were flying over a cloudy day on the way back. Through the white tissue-like vapor were the verdant valleys of Fishlake National Forest receiving rainfall. It was the first sign of moisture in a month, except for the welling tears behind sunglasses I wore to hide such embarrassing moments. Thoughts of losing Jeannette were overwhelming.

There was a dark and foreboding sense of failure in the atmosphere that I was forced to accept. The gambling junket proved depressingly scary, and Rusty was desperately broke, probably unable to bail the paper out of debt. Soon I'd be out of a job, forced to leave everything behind.

Nevertheless, I had three seats to myself on the trip home. Rick, the paramedic I rode out with, would also have a row of his own on the half-empty plane.

Rusty had driven me to the airport and said he'd be staying at Elaine's. He was going be working on a new business deal with Saville. Maybe get the paper functioning again. And I could be back to work, writing the piece about Blanche Banyan playing a major role in Derrick's death.

Fat chance there'd be a paper to publish it, although I relished the opportunity to expose the trip's perverse nature. Whether the story on Banyan followed a *National Enquirer* or *New York Times* style didn't matter. It would have been interesting; waging another battle against passivity. I'd follow all the clues wherever they led. I suspected it was back to Banyan's compound.

Earlier, when I boarded the plane, I had spotted Paramedic Rick on the way to my row. He looked up as I walked down the aisle. His big head with short-cropped blonde hair was easy to spot. He had a bulging neck and biceps overlapping the seat. As I approached, he glanced down, avoiding my acknowledgment, and flipped through a magazine impatiently. What pomp and arrogance, I couldn't help thinking. Although I've always admired those who came to the service of others, especially the medical profession, I didn't want to be treated with indifference.

On another level, I did sympathize with Rick. He looked as angry and melancholy as most people on the flight. No doubt he had lost a part of his life savings from a scam with the ironic claim he was the winner of a free trip.

"Any luck?" I asked, standing above his massive frame, and tossing my bag in the overhead compartment opposite his. My seat was still four rows back, but I didn't want to be ignored by the big lug.

"Not really. You?"

"I haven't calculated all the losses yet." He went back to flipping pages of his magazine. Another brush off.

I slammed the compartment door down, hoping to get a rise out of him.

Rick looked up, annoyed by the intrusion. Then he went back to tearing through the pages like a human magazine shredder.

"Sorry to bother you, but we're thinking of doing a story about the paramedic's procedure when responding to serious accidents."

"You'll have to talk to my supervisor." He leaned back and closed his eyes to any more disturbances.

I opened the overhead bin again and took out my bag, then quietly closed the compartment. Rick sat completely motionless except for his eyelids, which opened showing a blank stare.

I really didn't want to disturb him again and walked back to my row, chose the window seat and eventually fell asleep.

24

The plane landed at about two in the afternoon. Before I was fully awake, the paramedic was already out of the hatch. There were more questions I wanted to ask, like what happens to a person who is given a large quantity of poison before getting banged on the brain in a wreck? However, there were only a few people lingering outside the terminal in the scorching black-top parking lot, and the paramedic wasn't one of them.

The sun beat down with a blinding glare as I drove down Progress Avenue into a desolate downtown. It was Sunday, when everybody evacuated Great Valley. Still I was hoping to see some form of life, like Jeannette's car parked in front of *The Beacon*'s office.

I drove past the office in slow motion. It was dark inside, so I kept moving in the direction of home, to a motel room without any more opportunities with Jen.

"No messages," said Eloy Munn, who sat behind the counter.

When I got back to the room, I phoned Jim Tucker, hoping he'd know where Jeannette was, but he wasn't home, explained his wife. "I'll tell him you're trying to reach him," she said.

I hung up and waited patiently for his call before falling into a comatose state. Tucker later explained he had tried twice before I finally answered, two hours later.

"Jen's not coming back to work," said Tucker after finally waking me from the dead. Jeannette had phoned Tuck the day before with most of the details. "Jen found a bunch of delinquent tax notices on Rusty's desk. She was mad as hell and said that was the last straw. She quit, left her hubby and went to see her aunt in Crescent City."

"You got the number?"

"Yeah, but she sounded really upset and told me not to give it out, especially to you."

"Of course she didn't mean it, Tuck. We're old pals." I was practically begging for the number, but knew I could find it in the phone book as a last resort.

"I don't think it will help." Tuck lowered his voice until it was barely audible. "She says it's over."

"What's over?" I said.

"This isn't about you or her. She's mad because they're going to shut down the *Beacon* for back taxes."

I felt relieved it was about taxes and not a diluted relationship. The tax problem was a good diversion to the heartache I wasn't about to express over the phone.

263

"When Rusty gets back, hopefully he can pull things together. If he can't, we're shit out of a job. What's he doing out there?" said Tucker.

"Working on some business deal with Saville, if that makes you feel better."

"Oh yeah. See if he shows up with something more than the shirt on his back."

I didn't call Jeannette, deciding to take Tucker's advice and let tempers cool. There was nothing more to do but simmer down as the late afternoon sun beat through the west-facing window. The air conditioning rattled loudly, so I flipped on the TV to drown it out.

Sleep came easily at first, but after fifteen minutes the roar of an auto race on ESPN reminded me that life as I knew it in Great Valley was about to crash and burn, and I'd be behind the wheel heading back to Las Vegas. It was a gut feeling, a premonition that could be completely false if there was a chance to connect again with Jen.

I listened for the phone, but gave up and headed to the lobby for ice and eventually an encounter with a strong scotch on the rocks. Eloy Munn eyed me suspiciously, then cleared his voice: "Hey, Spiver, something I've been meaning to ask you." He was wearing a blue-gray uniform-type shirt and pants that blended with his skin. I walked over to the counter to pay my respects and rent, assuming that's why he had called me over. "How long are you planning on staying?" he asked. "I got reservations need filling."

"I'll start looking for a place," I told him, but didn't mean it. I wouldn't bother finding another room. Once I checked out, I'd be leaving Great Valley forever because there wasn't anywhere else to live in a town where rejection hurt so much it felt like a panic storm about to blow me back across the desert.

The prevailing winds were toward Las Vegas, where, behind the gleaming exteriors of high-and-low-rise hotels, the wounded gathered with their obsessions.

Yet there weren't any other choices. In a round-about way, somewhere between Great Valley and Nevada, was the truth I was looking for. The first stop would be to see Jen in Crescent City, then, no doubt, to some seedy spot where a lot of hopes and dreams were deposited in slots. I was hoping Rusty Gates had won big.

When I got back to Great Valley I was broken-hearted and broke. My chance to uncover a murderer disappeared like Rusty, who had skipped out on the show before the ending. And so Banyan's murder was another story that would go untold. There wouldn't be any justice when the audience was no longer in attendance.

After several more scotches with warm water, I fell into a Sunday-night-comfort-zone so deep it took an early morning phone call to arouse my spirit.

It was Tucker, calling from Joe's Doughnut Hut. "Wily, you heard from Rusty?"

"No. He probably won't be back."

"You better get down here. Meet me at Joe's when you get your rear gear in motion. And hurry, will you, I think we've had a permanent staff cut."

I sat across the table from Tucker gulping coffee like old times in editorial meetings. Only this time Jeannette and Rusty didn't attend.

"Tuck, you know there's no hope of salvation."

"And there's no hope if Rusty can't pay the taxes."

Afterward, we crossed the street and stood before the paper's front door. Barring our way into the office were the Department of Revenue's chains. The Department had come calling on Progress Avenue with a property seizure sticker and a strong lock for the entire world to see.

"I think keeping up appearances got to be too costly for the old Gates-ter," said a despondent Tucker. "Once Rusty lost the veneer, he might as well be in Vegas where it doesn't matter who you are."

Tucker and most of the staff stood at the front door and read the delinquent tax notice more than once. I hung back and waited for Tucker to finish telling everyone the party was over. When the mob disbanded, I pulled Tucker aside. "Tuck. I'm heading back to Las Vegas. Got some unfinished business myself. I'm going to try connecting with Jen on my way. Here's the scoop. Lucy found Blanche Banyan's Smart Phone at the accident scene a little while back. It indicates she was the one who poisoned Derrick for a bunch of money. I'm going to drop the phone off with Higgins. Maybe you can do a follow–up story if there's a market. Good Luck. I'll call you when I get a new cell."

"Good luck," he said.

We said our farewells and I went back to the motel to pack.

Before I headed out of town I dropped off the cell phone for Chief Higgins to analyze. "Wily, what the hell do I need another cell phone for?"

I told him I found it along the road where Banyan had the accident. "It might have some pertinent information about his death. And I'd like Jim Tucker to do a story about it if it ever becomes part of an investigation."

"What's that supposed to mean? Is that some of the evidence you and Lucy were withholding at the accident scene?"

"I didn't know at the time it was evidence." I really didn't want to discuss it any further. "If I can be of assistance let me know. I'll call when I get my new phone number. Right now it's just a lost and found item that I'm turning in to you guys."

Seventy miles west of Great Valley I cruised the hot deserted streets of Crescent City in search of Jen's aunt's house. I had found the address in the phone book and called from a convenience store in town to give her fair warning. She had agreed to see me for a few minutes.

Jen stood on the screened front porch of her aunt's cream-colored clapboard home wearing a tee shirt and jeans. Although it was hot, she looked cool and subdued. She also looked tired and frail. Her once creamy skin was pale and she seemed withdrawn, not wanting to go beyond the necessary boundaries.

She said her reticence came partly from her aunt's presence in the house, along with the stigma attached to leaving her husband and the unraveling of our plight in Great Valley.

A smile appeared between compressed lips in a sad sort of way and she used words sparingly. "Wily, it's all right. That's the way it is. I'm going to take a break from this whole mess. I need time to sort everything out."

And that's the way it was.

"It's just not the right time or place for us to be together."

I asked: "What's up with hubbie?"

"It's all but over for us. I'll be here for a month or so pending a divorce, I guess."

"Then what?"

"I'll probably check out the *Crescent City News.* They were always trying to hire me."

"Then maybe the truth about Banyan's murder will be told."

"Will you come back to write it?"

"I'll always be around for you."

"Give me a break," she said with a delicate smile. "You ought to try working for a greeting card company as a career move." Jen began to brighten a little, as if there was still hope for us.

Somewhere among the natural surroundings were the distorted chimes from a comical-looking ice cream jeep. It played the sad refrain of 'Doctor Zhivago' and our attention was held until the pictures of cartoon characters eating ice cream bars and Popsicles rolled slowly past the house and down the block.

"Wily, I got to go." Jeannette moved forward and wrapped her arms around me. Her head rested against my chest and I buried my face in her lightly fragrant hair. Between quiet, short breaths, her last words were: "Wily, let's stay in touch." She backed away, receding behind the door and waving before shutting it tightly.

Two weeks later I called Jim Tucker and he told me that Blanche's sister was arrested after they found traces of *cicuta maculata* in the compost pile behind the greenhouse. It was a form of water hemlock. The roots contain a complex alcohol, which in small doses causes death. Results of an autopsy on Blanche were still pending. "The foreman found the body after he noticed an arm floating on the surface of the river and called the cops."

I said to Tucker, "Do you remember the last time I was at the Banyan ranch, Blanche's sister served me some kind of concoction she said was their own brand of herbal tea. It tasted horrible even with a load of sugar in it so I only took a small sip. Later I got extremely ill and even had hallucinations. I kept thinking of it as some kind of witches' brew, like hemlock or something," I explained while trying to recall that dreadful event. "I always thought it was Blanche wanting to poison me."

Tucker said, "So Blanche's sister was the killer."

"Why not? She stood to inherit everything, especially that thousand-acre ranch that's got to be worth a fortune. Along with a pile of dough that Blanche and Derrick had from their environmental lobbying efforts. And besides, Saville told me the Banyans owned a couple thousand acres adjoining the Sorrow Creek area as part of their natural conservation plan. It was their way of protecting the land from oil and gas companies."

In the end, I always wondered if Derrick Banyan could have influenced the future of Sorrow Creek Basin. Or was Saville so alien to the area he scared off his allies, and that's why the concept of stealing water died a slow death.

Whatever the case, Banyan's legacy could live on for a few more years, that is until Sorrow Creek would actually be developed. Because in the long run, greed always seems to trump the necessity to protect the natural surroundings.